"I'm here to stay, Lizzie-bee," Eli said.

"Don't call me that." Lizzie's lips pursed with disapproval and tears shimmered in her eyes.

Lizzie-bee.

He held perfectly still, wishing he hadn't used his pet name for her. It had slipped out. How he wished he could go back in time and mend the rift between them. That they could be friends again.

"You are welcome here on our farm, Eli Stoltzfus, but don't expect anything else. I don't trust you anymore and that's that." She whirled around and headed toward the house, plodding over the wide furrows of alfalfa with singular purpose.

I don't trust you anymore.

Her words rang in his ears like the tolling of a bell. He watched her go, his heart plummeting. More than anything, he longed for a friend to confide in. But it obviously wouldn't be Lizzie. Not only had he lost her friendship, but he'd also lost her confidence and there was no going back.

Leigh Bale is a *Publishers Weekly* bestselling author. She is the winner of the prestigious Golden Heart® Award and is a finalist for the Gayle Wilson Award of Excellence and the Booksellers' Best Award. The daughter of a retired US forest ranger, she holds a BA in history. Married in 1981 to the love of her life, Leigh and her professor husband have two children and two grandkids. You can reach her at leighbale.com.

Books by Leigh Bale

Love Inspired

Colorado Amish Courtships

Runaway Amish Bride
His Amish Choice

Men of Wildfire

Her Firefighter Hero
Wildfire Sweethearts
Reunited by a Secret Child

The Road to Forgiveness
The Forest Ranger's Promise
The Forest Ranger's Husband
The Forest Ranger's Child
Falling for the Forest Ranger
Healing the Forest Ranger
The Forest Ranger's Return

Visit the Author Profile page at Harlequin.com for more titles.

His Amish Choice

Leigh Bale

Recycling programs
for this product may
not exist in your area.

LOVE INSPIRED BOOKS

ISBN-13: 978-1-335-50983-3

His Amish Choice

www.Harlequin.com

Printed in U.S.A.

The Spirit itself beareth witness with our spirit,
that we are the children of God.
—*Romans* 8:16

Thank you to Janet Pulleyn for infecting me with the soap-making bug. I have had a blast learning and consulting with you on new colors and fragrances. And thanks to Paul for letting me invade your home on more than one occasion. You are dear friends. Now, where shall we go out to dinner next time?

Chapter One

Elizabeth Beiler set her last crate of honeycrisp apples into the back of the buggy-wagon and took a deep breath. Picking the fruit was hard work but she could never get enough of its fresh, earthy-sweet smell.

Brushing the dust off her rose-colored skirts and black apron, she adjusted the blue kerchief tied beneath her chin. Because she was working outside, she'd left her white organza *kapp* at home. She arched her back, her gaze scanning the rows of apple trees.

Finally, they were finished. Not that Lizzie begrudged the work. It brought her a sense of accomplishment and security. She was just tired and feeling jittery with Eli Stoltzfus's constant presence.

At that moment, he emerged from the orchard, carrying two heavy crates of fruit in his strong arms. His blue chambray shirt stretched taut across his muscular chest and arms. His plain broadfall trousers and work boots had dust on them. Wearing a straw hat and black suspenders, he looked unmistakably Amish. His clean-shaven face attested that he was unmarried. Lizzie was dying to ask if he'd had any girlfriends during the four years he'd been living among the *Englisch*, but kept her questions to herself. It wasn't her business after all. Not anymore.

His high cheekbones and blunt chin gave him a slightly stubborn look. With hair black as a raven's wing and gentle brown eyes, he was ruggedly handsome. Not that Lizzie also was interested. Not in this man. Not ever again.

As he approached, she turned away, conscious of his quiet gaze following her. She often found him watching her, his intelligent eyes warning that there was an active, gifted mind hidden beneath his calm exterior.

"Come on, Marty and Annie. It's time to go home," she called to her two sisters in *Deitsch*, the German dialect her Amish people used among themselves.

The girls came running, the long ribbons on their prayer *kapps* dangling in the wind. At the ages of ten and seven, neither girl was big or strong, but they were sturdy and a tremendous help on the farm. Their happy chatter also alleviated *Daed*'s quiet moods. He hadn't been the same since *Mamm* died almost five years earlier. The union of Lizzie's parents had been one of love. The perfect kind of marriage she had once dreamed of having with Eli.

"What are we having for *nachtesse*?" seven-year-old Annie asked, slightly breathless from her run.

"*Ja*, I'm starved." Marty was right behind her, biting into a crisp, juicy apple from the orchard.

"I'm going to make slumgullion," Lizzie said, thinking the meat and pasta dish was easy to make and very filling. "And we've also got leftover apple crisp from yesterday."

She was conscious of Eli adjusting the crates of

apples in the back of their buggy-wagon, no doubt listening to their conversation. He must be ravenous too, but he would eat at home with his parents.

"Yum! I'm so hungry I could eat Billie." Annie leaned toward the bay gelding and made gobbling sounds. The gentle animal snorted and waved his head. Everyone except Marty laughed.

"You couldn't eat Billie. He's a horse. Don't be *dumm*," Marty said.

"No calling names, please. Be nice to your sister," Lizzie reprimanded in a kind voice. "As soon as *Daed* gets here, we'll go home."

They didn't have long to wait. Jeremiah Beiler emerged from the orchard, walking with their *Englisch* truck driver. *Daed*'s straw hat was pushed back on his head. Sweat-dampened tendrils of salt-and-pepper hair stuck to his high forehead. Dressed almost identically to Eli, *Daed*'s long beard was a light reddish shade with no moustache, signifying that he was a married man, now a widower.

The truck driver nodded, said something Lizzie couldn't hear, then climbed into the cab of his tractor trailer and started up the noisy engine. A rush of relief swept over her. The back of the 18-wheeler was loaded with crates of apples from their orchard and the driver would deliver them safely to the processing plant in Longmont. Their harvest was secure.

Because of Eli.

As the truck pulled away, *Daed* turned and smiled at them, but frowned when his gaze met Eli's. Lizzie knew her father didn't approve of Eli. He feared the younger man's worldly influence on his children and had hired him only at the bishop's urging.

"You all did *gut* work," Jeremiah said.

Eli gave a slight nod, then went to hitch his horse to his buggy. Lizzie watched him for a moment. Out of the blue, he had returned just over three weeks ago, asking to be reinstated in the *Gmay*, their Amish community.

If he had been a full member of the church before his decision to live among the *Englisch,* his choice to leave them would have been seen as a breaking of his faith and he would have been shunned. But because he'd never been baptized into their faith, he'd been welcomed back with open arms, no questions asked. Just a blind acceptance that he really wanted to be here. But Lizzie wasn't convinced. Eli had broken her heart. Leaving her the day before they were to be baptized together.

When they'd been only fourteen, he'd proposed marriage and she'd accepted. But long before then, he'd whispered about attending college to learn more about science and biology. Their eighth-grade education had never been enough for Eli, yet she had thought he'd made peace with the life they had. The life they'd intended to share. Lizzie hadn't believed he'd really leave. At least not without saying goodbye.

Annie and Marty beamed at their father's praise. They all felt a great weight lifted from their shoulders. The warm weather was an illusion. When they'd first settled in Colorado eight years earlier, they hadn't realized the growing season was much shorter than their previous home in Ohio. A killing frost could strike at any time. With their apples picked, they could now turn their efforts to other pressing matters.

To the south, the alfalfa was ready for cutting. The

last of the season. They would store the hay in their barn to feed their own livestock through the long winter. *Daed* would mow it tomorrow. The weather should hold long enough for the hay to dry, then Lizzie would assist with the baling. Between now and then, she planned to bottle applesauce. They no longer needed Eli's help and she wouldn't have to see him every day. Though it wasn't charitable of her, she counted that as a blessing.

"*Komm*, my girls. Let's go," *Daed* called.

Annie giggled as her father swung her into the buggy. Marty scrambled inside with Lizzie. *Daed* gathered the leather leads into his hands and slapped them against Billie's back, giving a stiff nod of parting to Eli.

"*Sehn dich schpeeder,*" Eli called as he lifted one hand.

See you later? Lizzie hoped not, then felt guilty for being mean-spirited. The little girls waved goodbye, but not Lizzie. It still hurt her deeply to think that Eli had loved worldly pursuits more than he'd loved their faith and *Gott*. More than he'd loved her.

"*Heemet!*" *Daed* called.

Home! With a cozy barn and hay awaiting him, Billie had plenty of incentive to take off at a brisk walk. The buggy-wagon wobbled as they traveled along the narrow dirt road leading out of the orchard.

Glancing over her shoulder, Lizzie noticed that Eli had his horse hitched up to his buggy and wasn't far behind them.

When they reached the paved county road, *Daed* pulled the horse up and looked both ways. A couple of cars whizzed past, spraying them through their open windows with a fine mist of grit. Once it was clear, he proceeded forward, setting the horse into a comfortable trot along the far-right shoulder. Within minutes, they would be home. Marty and Annie leaned against Lizzie and yawned. The gentle rocking of the buggy and the rhythmic beat of hooves lulled Lizzie to close her eyes.

She awoke with a start as the buggy-wagon jerked forward. A sickening crash filled her ears. Apples went flying, peppering the road. Lizzie reached for Marty, but found herself airborne. Bloodcurdling screams split the air. The hard ground slammed up to meet her. Pain burst through her entire body, a lance of agony spearing her head. She cried out, then choked, the air knocked from her lungs. Her brain was spinning, her limbs frozen with stinging shock. One thought filled her mind. Her *familye*! She had to help them.

Lifting her head, she stared at the remnants of the wood and fiberglass buggy-wagon, strewn across the county road. The fluorescent slow-moving-vehicle symbol that had been affixed to the back of their wagon now lay broken beside her. In a glance, she saw a blue sedan parked nearby, the right front fender smashed in. She blinked as a teenage boy got out of the car, his eyes wide with panic. In his hand, he held his cell phone. Had he been texting while driving?

Lying below Lizzie in the ditch, Billie snorted and thrashed in his harness. Giving a shrill whinny, the horse lunged to his feet, the laces hanging limp from his back. The poor beast. At least he didn't appear to have a broken leg.

Lizzie wiped moisture from her forehead, then gasped when she discovered it was blood. She scanned the road, looking for *Daed* and her sisters. From her vantage point, she couldn't see any of them. Her vision swam before her. She couldn't focus. Falling back, she lay there for a moment, trying to fight off the woozy darkness, but despite her best efforts, it crowded in on her.

When she came to, Lizzie realized she must have fainted. She had no idea how long she'd been out. A rush of memory made her jerk upright, then cry out with anguish. Her entire body hurt, a searing pain in her head. She must get up. Must find her father, Annie and Marty.

"*Schtopp!* Just rest." A soft, masculine voice came from above her.

Blinking her eyes, she saw Eli kneeling over her. In a glance, she took in his somber expression filled with concern. He must have come upon them right after the crash.

"*Vie gehts?*" he asked in a soothing tone roughened by emotion.

"*Ja*, I'm fine. Marty and Annie. *Daed*. Help them," she said.

"They're all alive. The *Englischer* has called for help on his cell phone. An ambulance is coming from the hospital in town," he said.

"Where…where is my *familye*?" She sat up slowly to look for them, her head whirling from another dizzy spell.

"I didn't want the girls to see you until I was certain you were all right. They're very frightened as it is. I'll bring them to you now." He stood, looked both ways, then hurried across the road.

He soon returned, holding the hands of her sisters

as he crossed the busy road. He hesitated as a car and truck whipped past, swerving to avoid the debris scattered across the asphalt. One of the vehicles stopped and asked if they needed help. The *Englisch* boy went to speak with the driver.

"Lizzie!" Annie cried.

Both little girls fell into her arms, sobbing and hugging her tight. Cupping their faces with her hands, she looked them over, kissing their scratched cheeks, assuring herself that they were safe. Their faces and arms were covered with abrasions, their dresses soiled, but they otherwise seemed fine.

"There, my *liebchen*. All will be well," Lizzie soothed the girls for a moment. Then, she looked at Eli. "But where is my *vadder*?"

"He cannot be moved just now. He has a serious compound fracture to his lower left leg. I believe his tibia is all that is broken. I have splinted the leg and stopped the bleeding, then wrapped him in a warm blanket I had in my buggy."

A broken leg! But how did Eli know what to do? A blaze of panic scorched her. They'd already lost *Mamm*. What would they do if they lost *Daed* too?

"I must go to him." She tried to stand.

"*Ne*, just sit still a moment. There's too much traffic on the road and you are also hurt. I believe you have a concussion." Eli held out a hand to stop her.

Lizzie recoiled, fearing he might touch her. How could he know she had a concussion? He wasn't a doctor. Or was he? She no longer knew much about this man. Was four years long enough for him to go to medical school? She had no knowledge of such things.

She reached up and touched her forehead. A wave

of nausea forced her to sit back. When she drew away her hand, fresh blood stained her fingers. No wonder a horrible pain throbbed behind her eyes and her brain felt foggy. Maybe Eli was right.

"May I…may I wrap a cloth around your head? It's important that we stop the bleeding. I've already done all I can for Jeremiah," Eli said, his voice tentative.

"Ja," she consented, giving in to common sense.

She sat perfectly still as he removed her blood-soaked kerchief. Her waist-length hair had come undone from the bun at the nape of her neck and she felt embarrassed to have him see its length. It was something special she was keeping for her husband on their wedding night. Thankfully, he politely averted his gaze as he opened the first aid kit.

"Where did that come from?" She pointed at the box.

He answered without looking up. "My buggy."

"How do you know so much about medical care?"

He shrugged, his gaze briefly meeting hers. "I went through the training and am a certified paramedic. I'm specially trained to help in critical situations like this."

So, he wasn't a doctor, but he might as well be. Although she'd heard about Amish paramedics and firefighters working back east in Lancaster County and Pennsylvania, she'd never met one before and was fairly certain her church elders wouldn't approve. Higher learning was shunned by her people because it often led to *Hochmut*, the pride of men.

"Is…is that what you've been doing among the *Englisch*?" she asked.

He nodded. *"Ja,* it's how I earned my living."

So now she knew. He must have worked hard in

school to learn such a skill. She couldn't blame him for wanting to know things, but neither did she approve of him casting aside his faith for such worldly pursuits.

Eli cleansed her wound with an antiseptic towelette. His touch was warm and gentle as he wrapped her head with soft, white gauze.

"You will need three or four stitches in the gash." He gave her a soulful look, as if he could see deep inside her heart and knew all the hurt and longings she kept hidden there.

She looked away.

Sirens heralded the arrival of two ambulances and some police cars. Lizzie lost track of time as the officers set up a roadblock with flares and took their statements. She watched Eli untangle the harness and lead Billie out of the ditch. Speaking to the distressed horse in a low murmur, he smoothed his hands over the animal's trembling legs. He then salvaged the bruised apples and put the filled crates into his own buggy.

When the medics loaded them into the two ambulances, Annie leaned close against Lizzie's side, her eyes red from crying. "Is *Daedi* going to be all right?"

Lizzie reached over and took the child's hand. "The Lord's will be done, *boppli*. We must trust in Him to get us through."

As she spoke these words, she tried to believe them. If *Daed* died, could she forgive the boy who had caused the accident? Christ had forgiven all and she must do likewise, but she wasn't sure her faith was that strong.

"I'll look after Billie." Eli stood at the foot of the ambulance, holding the lead lines to the horse's halter. His expressive eyes were filled with a haunting unease, as though he were anxious to leave.

"Danke." Lizzie gave a brisk nod.

He stepped back and the medics closed the double doors. Lizzie laid her head back and closed her eyes. And in her heart, she carried a silent prayer that they would be all right.

The following day, Eli tugged on the leather leads as he veered Jeremiah Beiler's three draft horses slightly to the left. The big Percherons did as he asked, plodding steadily down the row of alfalfa as they pulled the hay mower. The low rumble of the gas-powered engine filled the air. Eli glanced at the position of the sun, unable to believe it was afternoon already. Another hour and he would finish this chore. Jeremiah's hay would be secure. It would take a few more days for the hay to dry, and then he would gather it into bales.

"Gee!" he called, turning the team to the right.

A movement brought his eye toward the red log house where Lizzie and her *familye* lived. Turning slightly, he saw her and two men heading toward him, stepping high as they crossed the rutted field. Even from this distance, Eli recognized the slant of Bishop Yoder's black felt hat. His companion was Darrin Albrecht, the deacon of their congregation. Both men were dressed identically in black frock coats and broadfall pants. Eli had gotten word of the Beilers' accident to the bishop late last night. No doubt the elders had come to check on Jeremiah's *familye*.

Lizzie accompanied them, wearing a blue dress and crisp black apron. As they drew near, Eli saw a fresh gauze bandage had been taped to her forehead, no doubt hiding several stitches from her visit to the hospital. She and the little girls must have just gotten home. He'd seen the *Englisch* midwife's car pull in the driveway an hour earlier. She must have given them a ride from town.

Sunlight glinted against Lizzie's golden hair, the length of it pinned into a bun beneath her starched prayer *kapp*. One rebellious strand framed her delicate oval face and she quickly tucked it back behind her ear. Her blue eyes flashed with unease, her stern expression and brisk stride belying her injuries. Eli was eager to hear how she was feeling and also receive news of her father's condition.

Pulling the giant horses to a standstill, he killed the engine and hopped down off his seat. As he walked the short distance to meet them, he rolled his long sleeves down his forearms.

"Hallo," he called.

He glanced at Lizzie, trying to assess her mood. Their gazes clashed, then locked for several moments. As always, he blinked at the startling blue of her eyes. Her expression showed a fierce emotion he didn't understand. A mingling of repugnance and determination.

"Guder nummidaag," Bishop Yoder said.

"It looks like you've been busy today." Deacon Albrecht surveyed the cut field, as though evaluating the quality of Eli's work.

After being gone four years, Eli was surprised at how easily farming came back to him. It felt good to work the land again. It felt good to be needed. Holding the lead lines in his hands as the powerful horses pulled the mower had given him a sense of purpose he hadn't felt since Shannon's death seven months earlier.

Thinking of his sweet fiancée made his heart squeeze painfully and a gloomy emptiness filled his chest.

"You have done *gut* work for the Beilers," Bishop Yoder said. "They will need the strength of a man on this place for a few more months, until Jeremiah is back on his feet. He will have surgery today and will be in the hospital awhile longer, until the swelling goes down so they can cast the leg."

Eli nodded, wondering what the bishop was getting at.

Bishop Yoder placed his hand on Eli's shoulder, his gray eyes filled with kindness, but also an intensity that couldn't be ignored. "I've spoken with your father. He agrees that you should work here for the time being, caring for Jeremiah's farm as if it were your own. But with this request comes a great responsibility and commitment to your faith. I know you have told me you are recommitted to *Gott*. Are you certain our way of life is what you want?"

Eli hesitated. With Shannon gone and his confidence shattered, he had needed to get away from Denver and all the reminders of her death. Here in Riverton, he hoped to find the peace he so desperately longed for and a way to forgive himself for what had happened.

His heart still felt unsure, but he was determined to stay the course and wait for certainty to come. He couldn't go back, so he'd have to find a way for himself here.

"I am." Eli nodded, his throat dry as sandpaper.

Speaking the words out loud helped solidify his commitment.

"I just spoke with your *mudder*. She is inside the house, almost finished bottling applesauce for Lizzie," the bishop said.

Eli nodded, forcing himself to meet the man's gaze. "*Ja*, and my *vadder* was here earlier this morning, helping with the milking."

"You all have been most kind." Lizzie stared at the ground, her words low and uncertain.

Eli felt a wave of compassion. "It's our pleasure to help. You would do the same for us."

Or at least, he hoped she would. Her manner was so offish toward him that he wasn't sure. When he'd left four years earlier, he'd written to her often, at first. Not once had she replied. That alone told him she wanted nothing to do with him. After a year and a half of trying, he'd finally moved on with his life, meeting and falling in love with Shannon.

"*Gut,*" the bishop continued. "Tomorrow at church, I will announce your plans to be baptized, so you can participate in the instruction classes again. They've already begun, but since you took them once before, I think we can catch you up. Then you'll be prepared for your baptism in a few months."

Lizzie looked at him and a rush of doubt speared Eli's chest. The last time he'd attended the classes, he'd been a rebellious kid and hadn't paid much attention. In those days, all he could think about was getting out of here. Was he ready for such a commitment now? Once he was baptized, there would be no turning back. But he had the next few months to decide.

"I'm happy to assist the Beilers," he said.

A sudden hesitation struck him. A quick glance in Lizzie's direction told him that she didn't want him here. Her expression held a heavy dose of disapproval. As if she thought he was tainted now, because he'd been living among the *Englisch*.

He'd loved her so much when they were teenagers, but he'd had to leave. Had to find out what the world could offer. He'd desperately wanted a *rumspringa*— that rite of passage during adolescence when Amish teenagers experienced freedom of choice without the rules of the *Ordnung* to hold them back. But he'd never meant to hurt Lizzie. In fact, he'd tried to get her to come join him. If only she had responded to his letters. Instead, each one had been returned unopened.

The bishop smiled. "*Ach*, we'll see you tomorrow then. *Willkomm* back, my brother."

Eli nodded, but didn't speak. A hard lump had lodged in his throat. He felt grateful to be here, but the reasons for the gratitude were murky. Was he truly glad to be back among his people, or was he just relieved to be away from reminders of Shannon? He'd talked to other paramedics who had lost a patient in their care, but it hadn't prepared him for the shock. And to make matters worse, the first patient he'd lost had been someone he dearly loved. Someone who was counting on him to keep her safe. And he'd failed miserably. That's when he realized how much he missed his *familye*. Seeking respite from the world, he'd come home. But thus far, peace of mind had continued to elude him.

Reaching up, he tugged on the brim of his straw hat where a letter from Tom Caldwell was safely tucked away. Tom had been Eli's former boss at the hospital in

Denver. His letter was a silent reminder of the *Englisch* life Eli had left behind. And though it felt good to be back in Riverton, whenever Eli thought of never being a paramedic again, a sick feeling settled in his gut.

"If you have faith, all will be well with your *familye*. Never forget that," the bishop spoke kindly to Lizzie.

"*Ja. Danke*, Bishop," Lizzie said, her voice holding a note of respect.

The church elders walked away, leaving Eli and Lizzie alone. A horrible, swelling silence followed. Lizzie looked at the ground, looked at the mountains surrounding the valley, looked anywhere but at Eli.

"You are truly all right?" Eli finally asked, peering at Lizzie's forehead.

"*Ja*, I'm fine," she said, briefly touching the bandage as if it embarrassed her.

"I didn't expect this." He gestured toward the retreating men.

"Neither did I." Her voice wobbled.

"Are you sure you're okay with me working here?" he asked.

She glanced at him. "I don't have much choice."

True. With her *daed* in the hospital and the bishop's stamp of approval, she would have to accept Eli's aid.

"I never meant to hurt you, Lizzie. I know I left rather suddenly," he said.

She snorted and stepped back in exasperation. "*Ja*, you sure did."

"I know I should have spoken to you about it first, but I feared you might tell my *eldre* or the bishop and they would have tried to make me stay."

"*Ach*, so you ran away. You took the coward's route and fled."

He stared in confusion. He'd been gone four years. Why was Lizzie still so angry at him?

"We were only fourteen when I first proposed to you," he said. "I'm sure you agree that was way too young for marriage. When I left, neither of us was ready to start a *familye*. If only you had come and joined me."

"To Denver?" she asked with incredulity.

He nodded.

"*Ne*, I would never leave my people. You knew that."

"But I had to go. I wanted a *rumspringa*."

"So, nothing has changed. You still seek the world." Her voice sounded bitter.

He snorted, feeling frustrated, but unwilling to explain about Shannon and all that he had recently lost. "Believe me, a lot has changed. I'm not the same person anymore."

"And neither am I, Eli. You're homesick for your *familye*, that's all. But before long, you'll get homesick for the world out there that you left behind. We don't drive cars, use electricity, or swim the inner net. You'll get tired of us and leave again."

Swim the inner net?

He tilted his head in confusion, wondering what she meant. Then, he chuckled as he understood her words. "I think you mean *surf the internet*."

She shrugged, her voice thick with conviction. "Whatever. We don't do that. Pretty soon, you'll become weary of our quaint, boring ways and leave again."

Oh, that hurt. More than he could say. Never had he considered his Amish people to be quaint or boring. In fact, quite the opposite. The science of farming tantalized his intellect. The hard work and life here was definitely far from mundane. It was always a challenge to fight the weather, improve their machinery and produce a better crop...especially in Colorado. He also loved the solitude of fertile fields and the camaraderie of belonging to the *Gmay*. He always had.

"*Ne*, I'm here to stay, Lizzie-bee." But his words lacked the conviction hers had held. After all, his memories of Shannon were in Denver. When she'd died, he'd wanted to leave, but now he missed going to their old haunts where they'd fallen in love. He missed her.

"Don't call me that." Her lips pursed with disapproval and tears shimmered in her eyes.

Lizzie-bee.

He held perfectly still, wishing he hadn't used his old pet name for her. It had slipped out. How he wished he could go back in time and mend the rift between them. That they could be friends again. He could use the comfort of a good friend to help him deal with his broken heart, still full of love for Shannon.

"For the help you will give, you are welcome here on our farm, Eli Stoltzfus, but don't expect anything else. I don't trust you anymore and that's that." She whirled around and headed toward the house, plodding over the wide furrows of alfalfa with singular purpose.

I don't trust you anymore.

Her words rang in his ears like the tolling of a bell. He watched her go, his heart plummeting. More than anything, he longed for a friend to confide in. Someone to talk with about Shannon and his loss. But it obviously wouldn't be Lizzie. Not only had he lost her friendship, but he'd also lost her confidence and there was no going back.

Chapter Two

"I like Eli. He's so nice," Annie said later that night.

Lizzie jerked, her fingers losing their grasp on the tiny rubber band she was using to tie off the end of Annie's braided hair.

The little girls had both had their baths and Lizzie was finishing their hair before going to bed. Each child sat on the wooden bench in the kitchen, the gas lamp above the table shining down upon their heads. Their bare feet peeked out from beneath the hems of their simple flannel nightgowns. The air carried a slight fruity smell from the detangler she'd used on their hair to get the snarls out.

"Eli is nice, but you can't like him," Marty said. She tugged the comb through a particularly stubborn knot in her own damp hair.

"Why not?" Annie asked, her forehead crinkled in a frown.

"Because he hurt Lizzie's feelings, that's why."

Both girls turned and looked at Lizzie, as if waiting for a confirmation.

"Of course you can like him." Lizzie laughed it off,

not wanting to explain how much she'd loved the man and how he'd broken her heart. Everyone in the *Gmay* had known they'd been going together and planned to marry one day.

"We can? You're okay with it?" Marty asked.

"*Ja*, it's not our place to judge," Lizzie reiterated, trying to believe her own words.

"But you were gonna get married to him. Emily Hostetler said he left you to become an *Englischer* instead," Marty said.

"You were gonna marry Eli?" Annie asked.

Lizzie inhaled a sharp breath and held it for several moments before letting it go. Hearing Eli's betrayal put so bluntly made her mind scatter and she had to regather her thoughts before responding. As he had pointed out, they'd only been fourteen when he'd proposed. Way too young to marry. Because they'd been so young, he hadn't taken it seriously, but Lizzie had. When he left, they were seventeen and she'd thought they would wed the following year. It's what they had talked about. But he'd obviously changed his mind—and hadn't felt the need to tell her.

"That was a long time ago. It was Eli's choice to leave. When the time comes, we each must make that decision for ourselves, but I dearly hope both of you will stay." She placed Annie's *kapp* on her head, then hugged the girl tight.

"I'll never leave," Marty said.

When Lizzie released her, Annie stood, her inquisitive gaze resting on Lizzie. "Is that true, Lizzie-*bee*? Eli really left you to become *Englisch*?"

Lizzie-bee. The nickname Eli had given her when she'd been barely thirteen years old because he thought she was always as busy as a bee. Back then, Lizzie had loved Eli to call her that name. Now, it was a reminder of all that she'd lost.

"Where did you hear that name?" Lizzie asked a bit too brusquely.

"It's what Eli called you when he came into the house to take Fannie home after she bottled our applesauce. You were upstairs," Annie said.

Fannie was Eli's mother and a dear friend. She was as generous as the day was long. It had hurt her deeply when Eli left.

Lizzie sat very still, looking at her two sisters. Marty had been six when Eli had left, so she undoubtedly remembered him. Annie had been only three. Lizzie didn't want to discuss what had happened, but neither would she lie. Nor did she have a right to speak ill of Eli.

"Is it true?" the girl persisted.

"*Ja*, it's true," she said, tucking an errant strand of hair beneath Annie's *kapp*.

The child's eyes crinkled with sadness. "But everyone loves you. Why would Eli leave?"

She said the words as if she couldn't understand why Eli couldn't love her too.

"He…he wanted other things, that's all," Lizzie said.

"Did he hurt your feelings when he left?" Annie persisted.

"Of course he did." Marty flipped her long hair over her shoulder.

"*Ja*, he did," Lizzie admitted. She didn't look at the girls as she parted Marty's tresses and quickly began to braid the lengthy strands. Perhaps it was good for her sisters to learn early that a man could break your heart.

"But he's back now. You don't need to have hurt feelings anymore. You can forgive him and all will be well. Maybe he'll even want to still marry you now," Annie said.

If only it were that simple. Right now, Lizzie didn't want to marry Eli. And she certainly couldn't believe Eli wanted to marry her—not after the way he'd abandoned her. But sweet little Annie had always had such a calm, quiet spirit. Honest and trusting, the girl always exemplified a childlike faith in the good of others. Lizzie never wanted to see that faith shattered. But more than that, Lizzie had to set a good example for her sisters. With *Mamm* gone, they deserved to feel safe and loved. They were both looking to her for guidance and she didn't want to let them down.

"The Lord wants us to forgive everyone. We should never judge others, because we don't know what's truly in their heart or what their circumstances are. Plus we each have our own faults to repent from," Lizzie spoke in a measured tone, believing what she said, though she still struggled to apply it to Eli.

Annie nudged Marty with her elbow. "See? I told ya so."

Marty accepted this without question and Lizzie breathed with relief. She quickly finished her chore. Upstairs, she tucked the girls into bed, feeling like a hypocrite. She told her sisters to forgive, yet she hadn't done so herself. But honestly, she didn't know how. Saying and doing it were two different things. Forgiveness wasn't as easy as it seemed. Especially when she'd been hurt so badly.

She secured the house for the night and turned out the kerosene lights. Alone in her room, she prayed for help, but received no answers. Lying in the darkness, she closed her eyes and tried to sleep, but her mind kept racing. If Eli hadn't left, they'd likely be married now. They would probably have one or two children too. How different their lives might have been. They could have been happy and in love and working for the good of their *familye*. Instead, she felt disillusioned and distrustful. But it did no good to dwell on such things. It would not change the present. Her *familye* needed her and that was enough.

Punching her pillow, she turned on her side and closed her eyes, gritty with fatigue. She tried to rest, but it was a long time coming.

In the morning, she felt drowsy and grouchy. Determined not to be cross with the girls, she kissed each one on the forehead to wake them up. She ensured they were dressed and sitting at the table eating a bowl of scrapple—a mixture of corn meal, sausage and eggs— before she lit the kerosene lamp and stepped out onto the back porch.

Crisp darkness filled the air as she crossed the yard. The chilling breeze hinted that winter was not far away. In the waning shadows, she tossed grain to the chickens, then gathered the eggs into a wire basket. When she went to feed the pigs, she found the chore already done, the trough filled with fresh water.

Oh, no. This could only mean one thing.

Turning, she went to the barn. A faint light gleamed from beneath the double doors as she stepped inside. A lamp sat on the railing of Ginger's stall. The chestnut palomino was old, but *Daed* still used her to pull the buggy when Billie was lame. Thinking Billie needed a few more days of rest, Lizzie planned to use Ginger today, to get to church. It was too bad they'd lost their larger buggy-wagon in the accident. Now, they'd have to use their older, smaller buggy.

"Easy, girl." Eli stood bent over the mare's left back hoof. He wore a plain white shirt and black suspenders, his nice Sunday frock jacket hanging on a peg nearby.

Releasing the animal's leg, he patted her rump as he stood up straight. Then, he flinched. "Lizzie-bee! You startled me."

She bit her tongue, forcing herself not to reprimand him. It would do no good. The name *Lizzie-bee* was too embedded in their past history.

"I came to feed the animals. I didn't expect you to be here today," she said.

He shrugged. "I figured you would still need help even on the Sabbath."

Leading Ginger out of her stall, he directed the mare over to the buggy. Glancing at the other stalls, Lizzie saw that Eli had already fed Billie and *Daed*'s six Percheron draft horses. And judging from the two tall canisters sitting near the door, he'd already done the milking too. It appeared he was taking his promise to the bishop very seriously.

"Have you eaten?" she asked, feeling obligated to use good manners.

"*Ja*, my *mudder* fixed a big meal for *Daed* and me. I'll have the horse hitched up in just a few minutes, then I'll drive you to church," he said.

He didn't look at her while he put the collar on the horse. Ginger stood perfectly still, knowing this routine by heart.

"That won't be necessary. You're very kind, but I can drive the *maed* myself," Lizzie said.

He paused, holding the saddle lacings in his big hands. "I… I don't think that's a good idea. You were nearly killed just a few days ago and I… I assured the bishop that I'd look after all of you."

His voice caught on the words and he turned away, but not before Lizzie saw his trembling hands. Or had she imagined that? Why did he seem so upset by the accident?

"*Ne*, you told him you'd look after the farm. That's not the same as driving us to church," she said.

He nodded, accepting her logic. "Still, I feel responsible for you. I don't want to have to tell Jeremiah that I was derelict in my duty."

Hmm. Maybe he was right. The horror of the accident came rushing back and she realized she wasn't eager to climb into a buggy again. If her fear distracted her while she was driving, it could put her sisters in danger. Perhaps it would be better to let Eli drive them for a time. But she hated feeling like a burden almost as much as she hated to depend on him.

"You needn't feel obligated. I've driven a buggy many times before," she argued half-heartedly.

"I know that. You're a capable, strong-minded woman, but I'd feel better if you'd let me drive today. Just until Jeremiah is out of the hospital." His gaze brushed over the clean gauze she had taped over her forehead. She hated wearing a bandage and would be glad when the wound healed enough to remove the three tiny stitches. No doubt, they'd leave a small scar to remind her that *Gott* had saved her *familye*'s lives.

"*Komm* on, let me drive you," he said, his voice coaxing.

Oh, she knew that look of his. The calm demeanor. The slightly narrowed eyes. The softly spoken words and stubborn tilt that said he was going to do what he wanted one way or the other. Some things never changed.

But *she* had changed. Those soft feelings for Eli had been put away, and she wouldn't fall back into old habits, like smiling at him when he behaved this way. It was time for this conversation to end.

"All right, you can drive today. I'll go get the *kinder.*" She picked up a canister of milk and lugged it across the yard toward the well house. Fed by a cold mountain stream coming out of the Sangre de Cristo Mountains, the stone bath had been built by *Daed* when the *familye* first moved to Colorado.

Once inside, Lizzie set the heavy can into the chilled water and realized her hands were shaking from her exertions. When she turned, she found Eli right behind her with the second can.

"They're too heavy for you to carry," he said.

Yes, they were, but she could manage. With her father gone, she'd do whatever she must. Feeling suddenly awkward, she scooted out of Eli's way as he placed the second canister into the water bath.

"*Danke,*" she said before hurrying to the house.

The girls were standing on the front porch waiting, their *kapps*, dresses and aprons neatly in place. They smiled, looking so sweet and innocent that a feeling of overwhelming love filled Lizzie's chest.

"We even washed the breakfast dishes," Annie said

with a big smile, handing Lizzie the basket they would take with them.

"You did? You're so helpful." Lizzie smiled back, wiping a smudge of strawberry jam away from the girl's upper lip.

The clatter of hooves caused them all to turn. Eli drove the buggy toward them, his straw hat, vest and jacket now in place. Inwardly, Lizzie took a deep, startled breath. He looked more handsome than a man had a right to be and it pierced her to the core.

As he pulled Ginger to a halt and hopped out of the buggy, Annie scurried behind Lizzie, as if to hide.

"*Ne*, I don't want to ride in the buggy. Can't we walk today?" the child asked, gripping folds of Lizzie's dress as she peeked around her legs with caution.

"*Ja*, I would rather walk today too." Marty's eyes were also creased with fear as she sidled up against Lizzie.

Taking both girls' hands in her own, Lizzie knelt in front of them to meet their eyes. "It's too far to walk, *bopplin*. We'll have to ride. But I will be with you and the Lord will make sure we are safe."

Annie shook her head, her breathing coming fast, as though she'd been running. Lizzie knew a panic attack when she saw one. She pulled both girls into her arms and gave them a reassuring hug.

Eli stepped up onto the porch, removed his straw hat and crouched down so he could meet Annie's gaze. "Ginger is an old, gentle horse and she can't go very fast. You like her, don't you?"

"*Ja*." Annie nodded.

"And you trust me, right?"

A pause, then another nod.

"Then I promise to pull far over onto the shoulder of the road and drive extra careful so we don't have another accident. If I hear a car coming up fast behind us, I'll pull completely off the road until they have passed us by. I'll take good care of all of us, this I promise," he said.

A long silence followed as Annie drew her eyebrows together, signaling that she was thinking it over. Lizzie didn't know what she'd do if her sisters refused to get into the buggy. It was eight miles to the Geingeriches' farm—and eight miles they'd have to travel back. If they walked, they would arrive late, sweaty and tired. And the evenings were too chilly to walk home late at night. But she hated Eli's word choice. There had been a time not so long ago when she had trusted him and he had made promises to her too. Promises she'd naively believed with all her heart... until he'd broken them.

"All right. We will ride," Annie finally said in a tone of resignation.

Eli smiled wide, placed his hat back on his head, then picked the girl up. Taking Marty's hand, he walked with them to the buggy and set them gently inside. Lizzie was right behind them. Watching his tenderness with her sisters brought a poignant ache to her heart. Without Lizzie asking, he helped her into the carriage too, holding on to her forearm a bit longer than necessary. The warmth of his hand tingled over her skin and she pulled away as quickly as possible.

When he was settled in the driver's seat, he took the leather reins and slapped them against the palomino's back.

"Schritt," he called.

The horse walked forward, settling into an easy trot.

Sitting stiffly in her seat, Lizzie adjusted her long skirts and scrunched her knees as far away from Eli's as possible. She thought about her discussion with him the day before. He'd said he wanted to stay in Riverton. That he wanted to live the Amish way of life. But what if he changed his mind? She told herself she didn't care. He meant nothing to her now except that he was a member of the *Gmay*. So why did the thought of him leaving again make her feel so sad and empty inside?

Eli turned off the pavement and headed down the dirt road leading to the Geingeriches' farm. Another buggy and horse were right in front of them, with several more following behind in a short convoy. Eli followed their pace. Each *familye* waved and greeted one another like the best of friends. A faint mist had settled across the valley, but he knew the morning sun would soon burn it off and all would be clear by late afternoon when they began their journey home.

His parents should already be here. Joining them for meetings made him feel almost normal again. They were so happy to have him home that he felt good to be here. But he still couldn't help wondering if he'd made a wrong choice by returning to Riverton. He wanted to be here. He really did. But he couldn't seem to get Shannon off his mind. Her smile. Her scent. The way she'd begged him to save her life the night of the drunk driving accident. And then the stricken look on her parents' faces at the cemetery when they had buried their only child.

When the white frame house came into view, Eli breathed a sigh of relief. He'd promised the girls they'd be safe on their journey to church and he was grateful that he'd been able to keep his word. Too many automobiles flew way too fast down the roads. With drivers talking on their cell phones or texting, he could understand why the Amish were nervous as they drove their horse-drawn buggies and wagons. What was so important on the phone that it was worth risking someone's life? He'd had a cell phone when he'd lived among the *Englisch*, but he'd only used it when absolutely necessary. He'd found them a poor substitute for building relationships face-to-face. He was just grateful that a worse tragedy hadn't struck the Beiler *familye* and Jeremiah would recover from the accident.

Turning the horse into the main yard, he pulled up where two teenage boys were directing traffic. A long row of black buggies had already been parked along the fence line. Eli waited his turn, then pulled up as instructed.

"I can unhitch your horse," one of the boys offered.

"Danke." Eli handed the lines over, watching as the two teenagers removed the harness in preparation of leading the mare over to a field where she could graze and water with other horses.

Eli helped the girls out of the buggy. He noticed how Lizzie avoided his hand by gripping the edge of the carriage. She didn't meet his eyes as she smoothed her apron, then reached back into the buggy for a basket that was neatly covered with a clean dish towel. He had no idea what was hidden beneath, but surmised it was something tasty for their noon meal later on. The thought of spending the day with Lizzie made him feel warm. If he hadn't gone to Denver, they probably would have married. They'd be taking their *familye* to church like any other couple. But then he wouldn't have met and loved Shannon, and he couldn't forget that she had meant the world to him.

"Lizzie!"

A young woman with golden hair was busy spreading a cloth over one of the long tables set up outside. Eli didn't recognize her and wondered if she was a newcomer to the *Gmay*. She stood beneath the tall spread of a maple tree laden with leaves of bright yellow. The autumn air had a distinct crispness to it, but was still pleasant enough to eat outside.

As she approached, the woman arched her back, displaying an obvious rounding of her abdomen. Eli figured she must be about six months pregnant.

"*Guder mariye*, Abby. How are you feeling today?" Lizzie asked as the woman waddled toward them.

Ach, so this was Abby! Eli had heard all about her from his parents.

She rested a hand on her belly as Jakob Fisher joined them, taking her arm in a protective gesture. Before he'd left Riverton, Eli had known Jakob and his first wife, Susan, and their two small children, Reuben and Ruby. Jakob was older than Eli and they'd never been close friends, but Eli was sad to learn that Susan had died in childbirth while he was gone. Jakob had married Abby a year earlier and now they were expecting their first child together.

"I am well. The doctor has told me I'm perfectly healthy and should deliver just after the New Year," Abby said.

"*Ach*, you may deliver early. Wouldn't it be fun to have a Christmas baby?" Lizzie asked, her voice filled with jubilation.

Jakob smiled wide. "*Ja*, that would be the best Christmas gift ever."

Abby just beamed, her face glowing with an ethereal beauty that seemed to accompany every new mother as she worked hand in hand with *Gott* to create a new life.

"*Hallo*, Eli." Jakob nodded to him. "I would like to introduce you to my wife, Abby."

Eli smiled and nodded at the pretty woman. "I'm so glad to meet you."

"Likewise," she said. "I heard you are looking out for the Beilers while Jeremiah is laid up."

"*Ja*, the bishop thought it would be best," Eli replied with a half smile.

"Because of the accident, I heard in town that they're planning to put up more Amish buggy signs along the roads," Jakob said.

"*Ach*, it's about time," Abby said.

"*Ja*, that would be *gut*. I just hope it gets the drivers to slow down," Lizzie murmured.

Eli hoped so too. He hated the thought of any other members of their *Gmay* getting hurt.

The women stepped ahead of the men, moving off toward the kitchen. Marty and Annie joined Jakob's two children, racing across the front lawn in carefree abandon. Church Sunday was a time to worship *Gott*, but it was also a time to socialize and relax from daily labors. Both adults and children alike usually looked forward to this day with happiness. But not Eli. Not when he glanced over and saw several older women watching him, their heads bent close as they chatted together. He couldn't help wondering if he was the topic of their conversation, especially when Marva Geingerich eyed him with a look of revulsion.

"Don't mind old Mrs. Geingerich. She doesn't approve of anyone," Jakob whispered.

Eli jerked, realizing that Jakob had stopped walking and was watching him closely. "Does my nervousness show that much?"

Jakob nodded, his mouth turned up in a generous smile. "I'm afraid so. When my Susan died, Marva didn't approve of me either, simply because I was alone with two young *kinder* to raise. It didn't matter that I had no control over my wife's death or that I was grieving. Marva seems to be able to find anything and everything to disapprove of."

When Jakob put it like that, it sounded rather silly, but Eli didn't laugh.

"You must have been brokenhearted to lose Susan. How did you recover?" Eli asked, eager to know how to ease the gnawing pain he felt deep inside for Shannon.

"I'll let you know if I ever do. Right now, I doubt a person can fully heal from losing someone they have loved. But you have to keep living. And the Lord blessed me with a second chance at happiness. I never thought it possible, but I'm so deeply in love with Abby and I can't imagine living life without her." Jakob's gaze rested on Abby, his eyes filled with such wonder and devotion that Eli felt a lance of jealousy pierce his heart. Surely there would be no third chance for him.

Turning toward him, Jakob lifted a hand and rested it on Eli's shoulder before squeezing gently. "I know it couldn't have been easy for you to walk away from your *familye* when you left us, nor any easier for you to return. It took a lot of courage to come back and face your *eldre*. Now you have a second chance with Lizzie too."

Eli blinked, not quite understanding. For the first time since his return, Eli wondered if everyone believed he still wanted to marry Lizzie. After all, none of them knew anything about Shannon. But Lizzie didn't want him. Her words to him yesterday had indicated loud and clear that she didn't love him anymore.

"Facing my *eldre* was easier than you might think," Eli said. "They're both relieved I'm back. But Lizzie is a different story. I think I've burned a bridge with her that can never be rebuilt."

Jakob nodded. "No doubt she is still angry and hurt that you left, but she's refused to look at any other man since then. She has a *gut*, forgiving heart. With time, I'm sure both of you will be able to let go of the past, just as I did."

That was just it. Eli didn't want to let go of Shannon. How could he forget what she had meant to him and the part he'd played in her death? It was his fault she had died, but he didn't mention that to Jakob.

With one last smile of encouragement, Jakob turned and joined the other men as they lined up to go inside the spacious barn for their meetings. Eli followed, standing behind Martin Hostetler, who was three years older than him. With auburn hair, a smattering of freckles across his nose and blue eyes that gleamed with merriment, Martin was hardworking and filled with energy. Eli was surprised the man was still single.

Martin nodded and asked him several questions, but was cut off when they went inside, much to Eli's relief. His thoughts were filled with turmoil. As they trailed into the barn and took their place opposite the women, he considered Jakob's words. Yes, it had taken courage to return, and yet it hadn't been so difficult. Not when he'd been yearning for home—and everything in Denver had reminded him of Shannon, filling him with grief and guilt. But now that he was here, he feared he'd made a mistake. People in his *Gmay* would expect him to marry. And he couldn't do that right now. Maybe never. Perhaps he didn't belong in this world anymore.

He glanced at Bishop Yoder's pretty daughters sitting with Lizzie. The young women smiled shyly, then ducked their heads close together in a whispered conversation. Though he'd known most of them before he left, they all looked alike to Eli. Modest, chaste and pretty. With her creamy complexion and stunning eyes, Lizzie stood out among them, like a beacon of light in a sea of fog. Eli knew the Hostetlers and Geingeriches each had a daughter of marriageable age too, but he wasn't interested. Not in any of them.

He glanced at Lizzie, who stared straight ahead at the bishop. As the *vorsinger* called out the first note of the opening song, she opened her mouth and sang in German from the *Ausbund*, their church hymnal. How ironic that she was the only woman in the room who didn't seem to be looking at him.

Someone cleared their throat nearby and he glanced over to find his father's disapproving frown aimed at him. It didn't matter that Eli was a grown man. He was unmarried and still living in his father's household. Trying to refocus his thoughts, Eli joined in with the slow harmony, the words returning to his memory like a dear old friend.

Almost immediately, the bishop and deacon stood, then disappeared into the tack room to hold the *Abrot*, a leadership council meeting to discuss church business. While they were gone, the congregation kept singing, with no musical accompaniment. Eli stared at the closed door, trying to clear his mind and relax. Forcing himself not to look at Lizzie again. Attempting to push her from his mind. But it did no good. Again and again, he glanced her way, his thoughts returning to her wounded gaze. She'd made her position perfectly clear when the bishop had asked him to work on her farm. They needn't discuss the matter further. And yet, Eli couldn't fight the feeling that they still had unfinished business between them.

Chapter Three

The congregation knelt in silent prayer until Bishop Yoder released a discreet sigh. As a body, they each rose to their feet, turned and sat on the hard, backless benches. Once they were all seated, Lizzie watched as Bishop Yoder stood at the front of the room. With such a small *Gmay*, they had only one minister…Lizzie's father. And with him still in the hospital, the bishop would probably preach to them.

"What is in your heart today?" he asked the worshippers.

The question took Lizzie off guard. Tilting her head, she listened intently as the bishop spoke, his voice soft but powerful, like the sound of rolling thunder off in the distance. He met the eyes of each person in the room as though he were speaking to every single one of them. When he met Lizzie's eyes, she looked down, feeling suddenly embarrassed.

"Do you carry peace and charity within you, or do you harbor anger and malice toward someone?" the bishop asked, pausing to give them each time to search their hearts.

Lizzie squirmed on her seat. She glanced at Eli, but found him gazing straight forward, his expression one of thoughtful introspection.

Bishop Yoder lifted a book of scriptures. "But whosoever shall smite thee on thy right cheek, turn to him the other also."

Lizzie had heard this passage numerous times and thought she understood it clearly...until now. She had no desire to be hurt again and again, especially where her heart was concerned. But wasn't that what the Lord expected? For her to humble herself and cast aside her harsh feelings.

"Over the next weeks, I hope each of you will resolve any hard feelings you might carry toward others," the bishop continued. "Examine your own thoughts and actions and bring them into line with how the Lord would have you live. I beseech each of you to hand Him your anger and pain, your shortcomings and flaws. Then, once we all are in accord with each other, we will hold our Council Services in preparation for Communion."

Communion! A sacred time when the entire congregation must be in complete harmony with one another. With all that had happened recently, Lizzie had forgotten it was nearly that time of year.

As the bishop continued speaking about the rules of their *Ordnung* and the responsibility of each member of their community, she clenched her eyes tightly closed and gripped her hands together in her lap. Surely the bishop wasn't speaking directly to her. He couldn't know the resentment she still harbored toward Eli. Could he? Yet whether he could or not, she was the minister's daughter, after all, and she knew she should set a good example of love, tolerance and forgiveness. But how could she forgive Eli after what he'd done? He had soured her toward all men. She would probably never marry now. Never have a *familye* of her own. Never live in her own house. Over time, several men had asked her out. Martin Hostetler had pursued her doggedly, but seemed to have finally given up after the first year. Now it appeared she would become an old maid. Pitied by the other members of her community.

She took a slow breath, trying to settle her nerves. Her thoughts were selfish, she knew that. She was so worried about herself and what others might think about her that she hadn't stopped to consider Eli and his well-being. Why had he returned? What had happened to him after all this time? After he'd left, she'd been worried for him, fearing that he was lost forever. But here he was, seeking a second chance. And who was she to refuse him?

She had to find a way to let go of her anger. To forgive him. But how? All her life, she'd been taught the principles of repentance and forgiveness. So, why was it so difficult to exercise those virtues now?

Puzzling over her dilemma, Lizzie was surprised at how quickly time passed before they broke for the noon meal.

"*Komm* on. You can help me serve my potato soup." Abby spoke cheerfully as she took Lizzie's arm and pulled her toward the barn door.

"Potato soup?" Lizzie said, her mind still focused on the sermon.

Abby laughed. "I know it's a bit fancier than our normal fare of bread and peanut butter, but I'm feeling extra domestic lately. All I want to do is cook and clean. Jakob says I'm *nesting*. He says it's normal for a woman in my condition to act this way."

Laughing at Abby's enthusiasm, Lizzie let herself be pulled along. She could just imagine how fun it must be to anticipate her first child. But that thought brought her another bout of confusion, sadness and guilt.

Inside the kitchen, a dozen women crowded around, helping prepare the food. Their identical dresses were simple but pretty in assorted colors of blue, burgundy, purple and green. Each woman wore a pair of black, sensible hard-soled shoes, and a starched organdy *kapp*. Lizzie thought there was something lovely and serene about their simplistic dress.

Naomi Fisher stood slicing loaves of homemade bread in front of the counter while Sarah Yoder laid dill and sweet pickles on a plate. Abby stirred an enormous silver pot on the stove as Lizzie reached for a large serving bowl.

"I'll ladle the soup into the bowl and you can serve it hot to the men." Abby picked up a long ladle and dipped it into the frothy, white soup.

Lizzie nodded, sliding on a pair of oven mitts to protect her hands from the heat. Lifting the bowl, she held it steady while Abby ladled it full. The warm, tantalizing aroma made Lizzie's mouth water.

"Um, it smells delicious," Lizzie said.

"*Danke.* I crumbled bits of bacon and shredded cheese into it. It's one of Jakob's favorite dishes. It'll go well with Naomi's crusty homemade bread," Abby said.

"Did you see Eli Stoltzfus listening to the bishop's

sermon? I hope it sank in. That boy needs to mend his ways, that's for sure."

Lizzie looked up and saw elderly Marva Geingerich standing next to Linda Hostetler. The two women were unwrapping trenchers of sliced cheese and ham. Slightly deaf at the age of eighty-nine, Marva's rasping attempt at a whisper carried like a shout across the kitchen and everyone paused in their work. Especially Fannie, Eli's mother.

"*Ja*, I saw him. He's trying hard to fit back into the *Gmay* and doing a good job of it from what I can see," Linda said.

Marva's thin lips curved in disapproval. "*Ach*, I don't know why he ever came back. Once they leave and get a taste of the *Englisch* world, they never can get rid of it. I've seen it happen several times."

Something hardened inside of Lizzie. Though she was angry at Eli, she didn't like what she was hearing. It wasn't fair and it wasn't right.

"Marva! What are you saying?" Naomi paused in her slicing, her forehead creased with a frown.

"He won't stay long, you mark my words," Marva said. "As soon as that boy gets tired of living our humble way of life, he'll be off again to live among the *Englisch*."

"You don't know that. Eli returned of his own choosing. He wants to be here with us." Sarah Yoder, the bishop's wife, set a casserole dish on the wooden counter with a thump.

Marva jerked her head up, the wrinkles around her gray eyes deepening with her scowl. "*Ach*, he's been gone too long. Who knows what wickedness he's been up to? I don't know how he'll ever fit in with the *Gmay* now. No doubt he's got plenty to repent of. Mark my words, he'll leave again and that will be that."

An audible gasp filled the room and Lizzie flinched.

Turning, she saw the reason why. Eli stood in the doorway, holding an empty glass in one hand. His expression looked peaceful as a summer's morning, but Lizzie knew he'd overheard the conversation and must be upset. It was there in the subtle narrowing of his eyes and the tensing of his shoulders. Other people might not notice, but Lizzie knew him too well. For just a moment, she saw a flash of anger in his eyes, then it was gone and she thought perhaps she'd imagined it.

He cleared his voice, speaking in a composed tone. "I'm sorry to intrude, but Ezekiel has a cough. Could I trouble someone for a glass of water?"

Ezekiel, or *Dawdi* Zeke as most everyone called him, was the eldest member of the *Gmay*. Having just turned ninety-four years, he still had an active mind and was as kind and compassionate as Marva was harsh and unforgiving.

"Of course you can." Naomi, who was *Dawdi* Zeke's daughter, took the glass from Eli's hand, filled it with tap water, then handed it back to him.

"Danke." He ducked his head and left without another word.

Everyone stared in mortified confusion, not knowing what to say. A part of Lizzie felt compassion for Eli and the urge to run after him. But another part thought it was just what he deserved. That made her feel worse because it wasn't charitable to think that way.

"How could you say those things? It wasn't very nice. We should be more compassionate." Naomi shook her head, her expression showing her dismay as she gazed intently at Marva.

"I don't know what you mean. I only spoke the truth." Marva drew back her shoulders, pursed her lips and lifted her chin a little higher.

The hackles rose at the back of Lizzie's neck. Even if it was the truth, it wasn't kind. She would never consider belittling Eli to other members of the congregation on Church Sunday. It wasn't their place to judge him or anyone. Especially right after the bishop had preached to them about forgiveness and their upcoming Communion. But she couldn't help feeling like a hypocrite since Marva had voiced aloud her very same concerns.

Lizzie's gaze shifted to Fannie, Eli's mother. She had been cutting thick pieces of Schnitz apple pie but had dropped the knife onto the table when Marva had begun speaking. Looking at her now, Lizzie saw that her face had gone white as a sun-bleached sheet, her chin quivering.

"He's *mein sohn*. Do you really think he'll leave again?" she cried with naked fear.

Naomi quickly set her bread knife on the table before wrapping her arms around the other woman in a comforting hug. "*Ne*, it's nonsense! Don't you listen to such talk, Fannie. Eli fits in here with all of us just fine. He's one of our own and a welcome addition to our community. We love him and we're blessed to have him back. Look at all the *gut* he's done already for the Beiler *familye*. Isn't that right, Lizzie?"

Naomi looked at her and Lizzie blinked in stunned silence before stuttering over a reply. "*Ja*, he…he's been very kind."

"And who are we to judge others? We all have our faults. We are all happy that Eli has returned to his faith." Sarah nodded her approval.

"Danke." Fannie wiped one eye, showing a tremulous smile of appreciation.

"Humph! We'll see." Marva huffed as she carried a tray of sliced homemade bread outside.

Swallowing hard, Lizzie realized she was staring. Her mind whirled in confusion. Seeing the hurt on Fannie's face, she hurried over to comfort the woman.

"Don't listen to such talk. Eli loves you and Leroy. He wants to be here with you," Lizzie said, trying to believe her own words.

"But what if Marva is right? What if Eli leaves again? I don't know what I'd do. He's our only *sohn*," Fannie whispered.

A tremor ran down Lizzie's spine, but she fought off her own fears and tried to be brave. "If he leaves, we'll do as Christ taught and turn the other cheek. We'll exercise faith and face whatever comes our way and pray that he'll come back again. We can never give up on anyone."

Speaking these words aloud brought Lizzie a bit of courage. She meant what she said, yet her heart thumped with trepidation.

"I just don't think I can stand to lose him again." Tears shimmered in Fannie's eyes.

"We'll all be here for you, no matter what happens," Lizzie said.

Fannie nodded, but her sad expression still showed her unease as she returned to her chore of slicing pie.

Lizzie watched her, her own hands shaking.

Abby laid a hand on her arm. "Lizzie, are you all right?"

She gave a stuttering laugh. "*Ja*, I'm fine."

What else could she say? Only Eli knew if he would stay or go. Any member of their community could leave at any time, including her. Lizzie just wished she could be certain she wouldn't be hurt by his decisions.

"Don't worry," Abby said to her. "It'll be all right. *Komm* on. Let's get out of here. I need some fresh air."

Lizzie followed her friend outside, the screen door clapping closed behind them. They paused beneath the shade of the back porch. Children raced across the yard in a game of chase. Teenaged boys stood in a group, watching the teenaged girls. The afternoon sun sparkled in an azure sky. Lizzie wanted to cherish such a day…one of the last warm ones before the cooler weather rolled in. As she gazed at the rows of men sitting at the long tables, she let their subdued laughter soothe her ruffled feelings.

"I can't believe Marva said those horrible things. What was she thinking? She has such a waspish tongue," Abby whispered, her hands gripping the soup ladle like a hammer. "She's never been happy since her son brought the *familye* here from Ohio after his *vadder* died. She understands about repentance and forgiveness and should know better than to speak that way."

"Marva is rather stern," Lizzie agreed in a vague tone, once again feeling like a hypocrite.

"Jakob told me you and Eli were engaged once. I hope her words didn't upset you too badly," Abby said.

Lizzie shrugged as she gripped the serving bowl tighter, letting the soup warm her chilled hands. "That was a long time ago."

"Are you still friends with him now that he's returned?" Abby peered at her, as though looking deep inside her heart.

Biting her bottom lip, Lizzie couldn't meet Abby's gaze.

"Oh, Lizzie. I'm so sorry." Abby squeezed her arm. "His return must be difficult for you. And to have him working at your farm every day... But don't forget to keep an open heart and have faith. *Gott* will care for you both and all will work out fine. I know it will."

Lizzie couldn't manage to muster a smile in return. "I'm not so sure."

Resting her palm against her baby bump, Abby rubbed gently. "With my past history, I never would have believed *Gott* could make my life turn out so well. I thought I could never trust men and would never marry. But I soon learned that I was wrong. Give *Gott* a chance and He'll work so many blessings in your life, just as He did mine."

Lizzie understood. Since her marriage to Jakob, Abby had confided that she'd been physically and verbally abused by her father and elder brother. Abby was so happy now and Lizzie was glad. But she almost dropped the serving bowl when Abby turned and headed straight over to the table where Eli was sitting.

Breathing a sigh of resignation, Lizzie followed her friend, but couldn't help wondering if this day could get any worse. She wanted to turn the other cheek. To forget her pain and humiliation and believe that Eli truly was back for good. But she couldn't help thinking that Marva was right about one thing. Eli wouldn't stay.

* * *

"When did you cut your leg on the hay baler?"

Eli sat at the table next to Darrin Albrecht, their deacon. The autumn sun beat down on the men, but they'd each removed their black felt hats for their noon meal. They spoke in companionable friendship, waiting as the women set the food before them.

A rather hefty and somber man, Darrin was middle-aged with a thick head of salt-and-pepper hair and a long beard to match. As the deacon, it was his job to assist the bishop in disciplinary issues, to ensure that all members of the *Gmay* were following the rules of the *Ordnung* and to announce upcoming marriages.

"It's been two months since it happened and it wasn't even a bad cut. I can't understand why it's taking so long to heal," Darrin said.

Out of his peripheral vision, Eli caught sight of Lizzie standing just behind his left shoulder. She held a large, steaming dish, the aroma tantalizing. He leaned back, giving her and Abby room to scoop soup into his bowl. Along with the other women, they worked in silence, seeing to everyone's needs before their own. Glancing up, he saw Lizzie's face looked pale. She'd been in the kitchen earlier and he couldn't help wondering if she agreed with Marva Geingerich's opinion of him.

He clamped a hard will on his anger. When he'd returned, he'd known he might face disapproval from some of his people. It didn't change anything. He wanted to be here. And that meant he must exercise self-discipline, control his feelings and remain passive in the face of adversity. It's what the Lord would want him to do.

"Are you all right?" he asked Lizzie, worried that she and his mother were both overly upset by what had transpired.

"*Ja*, of course. Why wouldn't I be?" Before he could answer, she ducked her head and moved on to Deacon Albrecht's bowl.

Turning, Eli faced Darrin. "May I see your wound?"

He was conscious of Lizzie moving to the other side of the table as she served the other men, still close enough to overhear his conversation.

Beneath the table, Darrin hiked up his homemade pant leg to the knee. A gauze bandage had been affixed to the side of his lower calf with white tape. Eli ducked down and Darrin lifted the gauze to reveal a thin, jagged cut no more than an inch long. Though it didn't look deep, the wound was swollen and angry red.

"*Ach*, I have no doubt it's infected." Eli wasn't a medical doctor, but he recognized a septic injury when he saw one.

"Norma cleans it for me every day with hydrogen peroxide and ointment, but it doesn't seem to make any difference." Darrin pressed the bandage back in place and pulled his pant leg down.

Sitting up straight, Eli considered the man for a moment. "Have you seen a doctor about it?"

"*Ne*! There's no need for that. I don't trust those *Englisch* doctors." Darrin waved a hand in the air, then buttered a thick slice of bread.

Eli watched the man as he lifted his glass and smiled at Lizzie. Setting the serving bowl of soup down, she picked up a pitcher of water and refilled his glass…which Darrin had emptied for the third time since they'd sat down twenty minutes earlier. Several women from the congregation hovered nearby to keep the men's plates and glasses filled.

"You seem overly thirsty today," Eli said as he lifted a spoonful of soup to his mouth.

"*Ja*, he's always thirsty lately, even when he's not working in the fields." Linda Albrecht set a plate of sliced ham in front of them. She must have come outside while they were engaged in conversation.

"What about fatigue? Are you feeling more tired than usual?" Eli asked.

Darrin inclined his head. "Now that you mention it, I am more tired, even when I've had a full night's sleep. And sometimes, my feet feel numb too. Do you think the cut could be causing that?"

Eli took a deep inhale and let it go. This didn't sound good. "I'd feel better if you saw the doctor as soon as possible."

"That's what I suggested, but he won't go," Linda said, resting her hands on her hips as she tossed her husband an *I told you so* look.

"*Ach*, I'm fine. I'm sure the wound will heal eventually," Darrin insisted.

Eli met the man's eyes and touched his arm to make his point clear. "I think you're wrong, Deacon Albrecht. Please, go see the doctor. I don't want to alarm you, but you should ask him to test you for diabetes. If you've got diabetes, chances are it's probably keeping your wound from healing, which could cause other serious problems down the road. Don't take chances with your health. You want to be around to take care of your *familye* for many years to come."

Linda widened her eyes and pressed a hand to her chest. "Oh, my! Diabetes?"

Eli nodded. "He has some of the symptoms, but don't take my word for it. Let the doctor diagnose it for you. He'll be able to run some blood tests and let you know for sure. If the test is positive, he'll prescribe medication to control the problem. At the very least, he can ensure that wound on your leg doesn't turn gangrenous."

Linda gasped. "Gangrene?"

Darrin pursed his mouth, looking doubtful. Because Eli believed the man had a serious health problem, he pressed the issue further. "I'm dead serious about this, Deacon Albrecht. Go to the doctor first thing tomorrow morning. Please, do as I ask."

Darrin must have heard the urgency in his voice because his mouth dropped open. "You really mean it, don't you, Eli?"

Eli nodded emphatically. "I absolutely do. I want you to get some proper medical help."

"*Ja*, don't you worry. We will go first thing after our morning chores," Linda said. She was looking at her husband with a stern, wifely expression that would tolerate no refusals.

Knowing Linda would make Darrin go to the doctor, Eli felt relieved. He smiled and switched topics to the price of hay. When he reached for his empty glass, he caught Lizzie standing nearby. A disapproving expression drew her eyebrows together, but she hurried to fill his glass.

"*Danke,*" he said.

"*Gaern gscheh.*" She seemed both surprised and critical of what he'd told Deacon Albrecht. No doubt she disapproved.

She walked away and Eli longed to call her back.

To tell her of the extensive training he'd received in order to become a paramedic and that he knew what he was talking about. But these people would not be impressed. Nor did he want to sound boastful. After all, his training was from the Lord so he could serve others. It wasn't a matter of pride.

And he was glad he had it—and could use it to help the deacon. Though Eli wasn't positive Darrin Albrecht had diabetes, he was absolutely certain of one thing. If the man didn't get quality medical care soon, his wound could fester into gangrene and he'd lose his leg and possibly his life. But how could he tell Lizzie that? How could he explain that he only had the Deacon Albrecht's best interests at heart?

"Eli, if you're finished eating, will you help us out?"

Jarred from his thoughts, Eli turned to find Martin Hostetler standing next to him, a wide smile on his face.

"Come play volleyball with us. We need another player to complete two teams and, as I recall, you are good at it." Martin tossed a white ball high into the air, then caught it.

Deacon Albrecht smiled. "Go on, Eli. You'll have more fun with your young friends than sitting here with me."

Eli stood and turned toward the lawn. A net was tied across the grass, affixed to two long poles that had been cemented into old tires. Lizzie stood in front of the net. Seeing her, a feeling of anticipation zipped through Eli. Obviously she'd been recruited too. It had been years since he'd played volleyball...back when he and Lizzie were kids and still crazy in love with each other.

Walking over to the net with Martin, Eli glanced at the other unmarried people surrounding him. They seemed to be paired up on two sides. Some were as young as eleven years, while a few were as old as him and Martin.

Lizzie stood gripping her hands together, looking suddenly shy.

"Which side am I on?" Eli asked.

"You'll be on this side." Martin pointed to Lizzie's team and Eli saw her immediate frown.

She turned away, stepping to the back row, but Martin placed Eli right beside her. From where he stood beneath the shade of a tall elm tree, Bishop Yoder showed a satisfied smile. Eli couldn't help wondering if the man had rigged this to get him near Lizzie. Everyone knew they'd been engaged once. No doubt some of the congregation was trying to pair them back together. One look at Lizzie's wary gaze told him it wouldn't work.

She turned aside, seeming to focus on the other team as they served. She jumped gracefully, her hands fisted together as she struck the ball. From there, Eli knocked it easily over the net, scoring a point for their team.

Several of their teammates clapped their hands and cheered, but Lizzie stood silent. The ball was served again and volleyed back and forth for several minutes, then it zipped directly toward Eli. He hit the ball lightly, offering a layup to Lizzie, just like he'd done when they were teenagers. Instead of spiking the ball over the net, Lizzie jumped back and let the ball hit the ground. It rolled onto the graveled driveway and one of the younger children chased after it.

The other team cheered.

"Tied points," Martin called from in front of the net. Facing Eli, the redheaded man smiled wide, but there was no malice in his expression. He was merely having fun.

"I thought you would spike the ball, like you used to do," Eli spoke low for Lizzie's ears alone.

"I... I didn't see it soon enough," she returned, sounding slightly irritated.

Eli didn't know if she was flustered by his presence, or if dropping the ball was her way of rejecting him. He couldn't help thinking about what Jakob had said earlier. Did Lizzie still harbor resentment toward him for breaking off their engagement when he left all those years ago?

"Are you sure you're all right?" he asked her while the other team readjusted their positions so they could serve the ball.

"Of course, why?"

Yes, he definitely caught a note of exasperation in her tone.

He shrugged. "No reason, really. I just noticed that you seemed annoyed when I was speaking with Deacon Albrecht and now again."

Her slim jaw hardened. "You're not a doctor, Eli. But I can see you gained plenty of *Hochmut* from going to college. You seem to think you know what is good for everyone."

So that was it. Like many of their people, she didn't approve of higher learning. She thought he was too prideful.

"I don't think that at all. I only want to help, Lizzie-bee. That's why I told Deacon Albrecht to go see a doctor as soon as possible…so he can get an accurate diagnosis," he said.

Releasing a heavy sigh, she turned away and focused on the game. She did an admirable job of ignoring him. No doubt she agreed with Marva Geingerich, that he would leave again. And how could he persuade her that he really wanted to stay in Riverton when he hadn't yet convinced himself?

They won the game, but Lizzie hurried off to help in the kitchen before a second match began. Karen Hostetler, who was Martin's eighteen-year-old sister, and Ellen Yoder, the bishop's daughter, both smiled prettily at him. In between serving the ball, they engaged Eli in conversation. He tried to show interest, but his gaze kept roaming over to the house where he sought some sight of Lizzie. After the second game ended, the teams broke up. Eli was glad. He had no interest in playing volleyball. At least, not without Lizzie.

He didn't see her again until it was time to drive her and the little girls home that evening. Though he wanted to head back before it got too late, he had to stay a little longer so he could attend the instruction class with the two others who were planning to be baptized in a few months. As Eli listened to the lesson from Bishop Yoder, he liked what he heard, but felt a bit nervous when he considered its importance. Once he was baptized into the Amish faith, his life would change forever. He would not take the vows unless he was absolutely confident that he intended to live them for the rest of his life.

On their way home, Marty and Annie were eager to chat about their day. As the buggy moved along at a rapid pace, Lizzie sat quietly with her hands in her lap. Eli longed to talk with her about his class, to get her opinion on several issues, but whenever he tried to engage her in conversation, her response was rather abrupt. Finally, he gave up trying.

As they pulled into the farmyard, dusk was settling over the western sky with clouds of pink, orange and gray. He looked up at the tall Sangre de Cristo Mountains and thought he'd never seen anything so beautiful in all his life. He had just enough time to milk the cows and head home to his parents before it turned dark.

"*Danke* for driving us safely," little Annie said.

"*Ja, danke* for keeping your promise," Marty agreed.

The girls both smiled and hugged him, but Lizzie simply nodded, then went inside the house.

Watching her go, a feeling of melancholy blanketed Eli and he wondered what he could do to improve her opinion of him. It seemed that she'd lost all faith in him, and he couldn't really blame her. But that's when he made a promise to himself. No matter how long it took, he was determined to regain her trust. He just wasn't certain how.

Chapter Four

By noon the following morning, Eli had almost finished raking the alfalfa. Dust sifted through the air as the two-horse hitch plodded along with the patience of Job. The tines connecting to the four horizontal bars of the side rake moved in a circular motion as they rolled the hay into straight, tidy windrows. The action also fluffed and turned the hay, so it would dry well before they baled it tomorrow. Eli was eager to get the hay in as quickly as possible. The unseasonable warmth wouldn't hold much longer. He figured they had one or two more days before the clouds rolled in and brought rain to the valley.

Glancing toward the farmhouse, he saw Lizzie outside hanging clothes on the line. They hadn't spoken since church and he felt the tension between them reaching clear across the field.

Annie was helping her older sister, lifting damp clothes out of the white laundry basket to hand over to Lizzie. Marty stood nearby, gathering seeds from the dried marigolds that had grown all summer long in the flowerbeds surrounding the house. Above the rattling noise of the hay rake, Eli could catch hints of the happy sound of their laughter.

The rake gave a little bump and he turned to face forward, focusing on his work. When he finished twenty minutes later, he pulled the draft horses to a halt, lifted the horizontal bars, then drove the Percherons toward the barn. Lizzie was no longer in the yard and he figured she'd gone into the house with the girls.

He deposited the rake in the barn, then cared for the horses. After watering the Percherons, he checked each of their hooves, bodies and heads. If one of them picked up a stone or had a wound of some kind, they wouldn't be much use in baling tomorrow morning. It'd take all six draft horses to pull the heavy baler and hay wagon.

Satisfied the animals were in good condition, he turned them loose in the pasture. Before he went up to the house for some lunch, he entered the cool shadows of the barn. Removing his straw hat, he wiped his forehead on his shirtsleeve and sat on a tall stool.

Another letter had arrived from Tom Caldwell, his old boss at the hospital in Denver. Pulling the short letter from the envelope, Eli read it one more time. Tom knew about Shannon's death and understood that Eli had been badly shaken by the accident. Tom had encouraged him to take and break and go home for a visit. But now, Tom was shorthanded and badly needed qualified paramedics. In his letter, he'd offered Eli a raise if he would return to work by the end of October. Eli had already sent his regrets. He was not at all certain he'd ever return to Denver—but he definitely wouldn't be going back that soon. After all, Jeremiah wouldn't be healed enough to work by that time and

Eli had given his word to the bishop that he would care for the farm until then.

"Eli?"

He jerked around, dropping the letter in the process. The paper wafted to the ground and he scooped it up, shoving it into his hat.

"What's that you're reading?" Lizzie stood in front of the double doors, holding a tray with a plate of food and tall glass of milk. A shaft of sunlight glimmered behind her, highlighting her in beams of gold.

"Nothing of consequence."

A flush of heat rose in his face. It was bad enough that his parents knew he was receiving letters and were worried his *Englisch* friends might draw him back to Denver. If only he didn't feel so conflicted. Helping Deacon Albrecht yesterday had felt so good and familiar, but he couldn't tell Lizzie that, nor his parents either. Not after what Marva Geingerich had said. They might judge him harshly. If only Shannon were here. She would advise him in that soft, understanding manner of hers. But if she were still alive, he would never have come home.

"Is it a letter?" Lizzie stepped closer, setting the tray on a low ledge of timber.

He placed the hat on his head. "*Ja*, a letter."

Her eyes crinkled with concern. "A letter from whom?"

"An old friend in Denver," he said, trying to sound unruffled.

She tilted her head to one side, her eyes narrowing. "An *Englisch* friend?"

He nodded, unwilling to lie. Except for his love for Shannon, it seemed he couldn't keep any secrets from this woman. When they'd been young, she was the only one who had known of his desire to go to college. She hadn't told a soul and, because of that, he'd thought she'd understand when he left. That she might even join him. But he had been dead wrong.

She took a deep breath, then let it go in a slow sigh. "What do they want?"

The moment she asked the question, she blinked and flushed with embarrassment. She lifted a hand to nervously adjust her white *kapp*. He almost laughed at the feminine gesture, unable to keep from admiring her graceful fingers, or the way her blue eyes darkened.

"I'm sorry. I shouldn't have asked that. It's none of my business. I brought you something to eat." She turned and gestured to the tray.

He cleared his throat, feeling like he'd swallowed sandpaper. "Was there…was there something else you wanted?"

She nodded, meeting his eyes again. "*Ja*, I was waiting until you finished raking the hay. I know that's the priority right now. But I was wondering if you might have time to drive the *maed* and me into town to visit our *vadder* at the hospital this afternoon."

Ah, so she still wasn't over the shock of the accident and still didn't feel confident enough to drive herself. He thought about teasing her, but sensed it was difficult for her to confide this weakness to him. Besides, he liked having something normal and mundane to distract him from the conflict waging a war inside his mind.

"Of course. I'd be happy to drive you and the *kinder*," he said.

"*Gut*. We'll be ready to leave as soon as you've eaten. I also wanted to stop off at Ruth Lapp's house. She wasn't at church because she has bronchitis, so I thought I'd take a meal to her *familye*. Nothing fancy. Just a casserole and some pumpkin muffins."

Yum! Pumpkin muffins. His mouth watered at the thought. He glanced at the plate she'd brought him, noticing she'd included a muffin with thick cream cheese icing for him too. "That's very kind of you."

In fact, her generosity reminded him of why he'd returned. Because he loved this way of life. The way his people looked after one another. Their generosity and devotion to what they believed was right. He realized that even old Marva Geingerich's biting comments were made out of fear that he might leave again, which would hurt those he left behind. A part of him wanted to stay, just to prove her wrong. To show the *Gmay* how much he loved it here.

"But I'll need to leave early tonight," he said.

"Oh?" She cocked an eyebrow.

"I need to drive to Bishop Yoder's house. He's helping me make up for lost time, so I can catch up with the other students planning to be baptized in a few months. I still need to read the articles of the Dordrecht Confession."

"*Ach*, you didn't read them the last time you took the classes, before you left?"

"*Ne*, I'm afraid not."

"Then of course you must go. That's very important. You won't want to be late. We'll only be gone long enough to pay a quick visit to *Daed* and drop off the meal," she said.

"*Gut*."

They gazed at each other and the silence lengthened. In the past, they'd never had a lack of things to say to each other. Even silences had been comfortable between them. But not anymore.

Putting her hands behind her back, Lizzie scuffed the toe of her shoe against the ground. "*Ach*, I guess I'd better get back to the house and get the *kinder* ready to leave."

"*Ja*, I'll bring the buggy out in a few minutes."

With one final nod, she whirled around and was gone, leaving him feeling suddenly very empty inside.

As Lizzie hurried to the house, she thought it might have been a mistake to ask Eli to drive her and the girls into town. It seemed silly that she couldn't drive herself. And yet, she still felt too nervous. But more than that, she hated to admit that Eli's presence brought her a great deal of comfort. She liked having him here and that was dangerous on so many levels. More than anything, she had to protect her heart. Because she couldn't stand the pain of loving and losing him again.

Within ten minutes, she had the kitchen tidied and the children ready to leave. Standing on the front porch with Marty, she held a large basket containing the promised meal for the Lapps inside. She'd also tucked a couple of pumpkin muffins in for her father, although she wasn't sure if he had any diet restrictions. If so, she'd give them to the nurses.

The rattle of the buggy brought her head up and she saw Eli driving Ginger toward them from the barn.

"*Komm* on, Annie. We're going to see *Daed*," Marty called excitedly.

Annie came running, a huge smile on her face. In

her excitement, she slammed the front door behind her. "*Ach*, I can't wait. It's been forever since we saw *Daed*."

Lizzie smiled at her exuberance and tugged playfully on one of the ribbons to her *kapp*. "It's only been a few days, *bensel*."

The child hopped on one foot with excitement. "It feels like forever. I can't wait for *Daed* to come home."

Neither could Lizzie. For some reason, she felt more vulnerable with him gone. More dependent upon Eli. She'd have to correct that problem soon. She couldn't rely on Eli forever.

They settled into the buggy with Eli holding the lead lines in his strong hands. There was something restive in watching him work with the horse. Though he displayed self-confidence, he was quiet and respectful, seeming lost in his own thoughts.

"When do you think Billie will be ready to drive again?" she asked.

He stared straight ahead as he responded. "Physically, I think he's ready now, but I'm not sure how he'll respond up on the county road. Tomorrow, I'll take him out alone, to make sure he doesn't panic when cars and trucks whiz by us."

How insightful. It hadn't occurred to Lizzie that the horse might also be skittish around motorized vehicles now. It figured that Eli was perceptive enough to realize this and considerate enough to drive the horse alone, so no one else would get hurt if the animal bolted.

"I appreciate that," she said.

He shrugged one shoulder. "It's no problem. I'm happy to help out."

Yes, that was just the problem. His kindness and generosity to her *familye* made it difficult to be angry with him. Yet, she didn't dare forget.

Marty scooted forward from the back seat and leaned against Lizzie's shoulder. "Do you think *Daed* will be able to come home with us today?"

"I don't know, *boppli*. I doubt it. We'll have to see what the doctor says."

Not to be left out, Annie nudged her way in and leaned against Eli. "How long will *Daed* have to stay in the hospital? I miss him."

Lizzie reached up and squeezed Annie's hand. "Like I said, we won't know until we talk to the doctor. I know we all miss *Daed*, but he's going to be all right and we'll see him soon. Now, sit back and give Eli room to drive."

Satisfied with this reassurance, the girls smiled and sat back. Eli glanced Lizzie's way and his soft smile made her heart skip a couple of beats in spite of herself.

Along their way, they stopped off at the Lapps' modest farmhouse to deliver the food. As Eli pulled up out front, Lizzie faced him.

"Since Ruth is so sick, will you keep the *kinder* out here with you, please? I don't want them to catch her illness. I'll only be a minute," she said.

Marty and Annie frowned, but didn't say anything. No doubt they were hoping to play with Ruth's children.

Eli ducked his head in assent. "Of course."

Lizzie nodded and hopped out of the buggy. When she reached back, Eli handed her the basket.

Moments later, Ruth answered the door. She was

fully dressed, but her apron was stained and slightly crooked. There were dark circles beneath her eyes, her hair coming loose from her *kapp*, and her nose was bright red. In one hand, she clutched several tissues. With her other hand, she bounced her toddler on her hip, the little boy holding a full bottle of milk.

"Lizzie! It's nice of you to visit." Ruth covered her mouth as she gave a hacking cough that sounded like it rattled something deep down in her lungs. "I don't dare let you in. I fear I'd only give you my cold and then you'd pass it on to your entire *familye*."

"You should try a humidifier. That might help you to breathe easier," Lizzie suggested.

Trying not to be obvious, she glanced behind Ruth, noting that everything inside the house looked in fairly good order. Two older children sat on the sofa, quietly reading books. The baby seemed well cared for too. Except that she didn't feel well, Ruth seemed to be coping and seeing to the needs of her *familye*.

"*Ja*, I have one running now," Ruth said.

"*Gut*. I won't stay, but I wanted to help in some way. At least you won't have to cook *nachtesse* tonight." Lizzie handed over the basket.

"*Ach*, that's so kind of you. You're a *gut* friend." Ruth took the basket with her free hand and smiled as she jutted her chin toward the buggy. "Is that Eli Stoltzfus I see in the buggy?"

Lizzie nodded, her senses flaring. "*Ja*, it is."

"You're back together then?"

Lizzie automatically stiffened. "*Ne*, he's just helping out at the farm while my *vadder* is laid up."

"*Ja*, I heard something about Jeremiah being injured. I'm so glad you and the girls are safe and hope

Jeremiah is better soon." Ruth set the basket on a table before shifting the baby to her other hip. "It'd be so nice if you and Eli got back together, though."

Lizzie didn't know what to say, so she chose to ignore the comment by smiling brilliantly. "If you need anything at all, you just let me know."

"I will." Ruth nodded.

"I'll check on you again in a few days," Lizzie promised, stepping down off the porch.

"*Danke* so much." Ruth waved to the occupants of the buggy before going inside and shutting the door.

Whew! Thankfully, Ruth didn't push the issue. Lizzie wasn't prepared to answer questions about her and Eli. They weren't getting back together, but it poked at old wounds to go around telling everyone that.

As she climbed into the buggy, Eli reached out and pulled her up. The grip of his hand around hers felt strong yet gentle. She quickly sat and smoothed her skirts before he clicked his tongue and the horse took off again.

"What you just did was very *gut*. You're a kind example for your *schweschdere*." He glanced back at the two little girls.

"*Danke.*" Lizzie didn't know what else to say. She hadn't sought his approval and yet she couldn't help feeling suddenly very happy inside. She told herself it was because she'd just done an act of service to someone in need, but she knew it was something more. Something she didn't understand.

They didn't speak for most of the remaining journey into town. Following the traffic light on Main Street, Eli pulled up in front of the hospital and climbed out.

As he took Lizzie's arm to help her down, he looked rather stoic. "I'll let you go inside to visit your *vadder* while I tie the horse."

Hmm. Obviously he wasn't eager to see Jeremiah. That suited Lizzie just fine.

"Danke." She beckoned to her sisters.

As they hurried up the steps, the automatic double doors whooshed open. Lizzie glanced over her shoulder and saw Eli back inside the buggy and pulling away.

Inside the small hospital, the air smelled of overdone meatloaf and antiseptic. Several people sat in the reception area, gawking at Lizzie and the girls. No doubt they found their Amish clothing a bit strange. Lizzie was used to such stares and ignored them as she approached the front reception desk.

"We're here to visit our father," she spoke in perfect English.

A nurse wearing a blue smock and pants smiled pleasantly. "Oh, I'll guess you're Jeremiah Beiler's daughters."

"Yes, that's right," Lizzie said.

"The doctor is with him right now. Room eighteen just down the hallway." The nurse pointed the way.

Taking Annie's and Marty's hands, Lizzie led them down the hall, the click of her shoes echoing behind. A man wearing a white smock stood just inside the room, a stethoscope hanging from his neck.

"Ach, here are my girls now."

Jeremiah lay in a hospital bed covered with a white sheet. His broken leg lay flat on the mattress, but cradled by pillows and a blanket.

"Daedi!" Both Annie and Marty ran to their father, hugging his neck tight.

He chuckled and kissed them each on the forehead. "I'm so glad to see you *maed*. Have you missed me?"

"*Ja*, something fierce, *Daed*," Marty said.

"And have you been *gut* for Lizzie?"

"*Ja, Daed*. We're helping her all we can," Annie said.

He laughed again and glanced at the doctor, who grinned at the two little imps. Lizzie smiled and nodded respectfully as her father introduced her to Dr. McGann. She'd heard good things about the man from other members of the Amish community. He wasn't pushy and seemed genuinely concerned for their welfare. Just the kind of man she wanted to care for her father.

"When can you come home?" Marty asked, her voice anxious.

Jeremiah looked at the doctor and lifted one hand. "You see? I told you I have a lot of support at home. Can't I go there to recuperate?"

Dr. McGann shook his head. "I'm afraid not yet. The swelling needs to go down before we can cast your leg. The orthopedic surgeon did a fine job in aligning the broken bones, but it was a serious break and you mustn't put any weight on the leg yet."

"How long will he need to stay here, Doctor?" Lizzie asked, wanting to do what was best for her father, but anxious for him to be where she could care for him.

"We'll have to see. Let's give it a few more days and go from there. Otherwise, your father is doing well and I see no reason why we shouldn't be able to rehabilitate his leg. But he won't be able to put any weight on the broken bones for at least six more weeks."

"Six weeks! So long?" she asked with amazement, thinking of all the chores awaiting them at home and how difficult it would be to keep her father down. Perhaps it was best for him to remain here at the hospital awhile longer.

Dr. McGann nodded. "I'm afraid so."

"Danke." Lizzie reminded herself that the results of the accident could have been much more serious.

Dr. McGann smiled at Marty and Annie. "Now, if it's all right with your sister, how would you two like a nice lollipop? I happen to know that Nurse Carter keeps a jar of them by her desk just for pretty girls like you."

The children looked at their elder sister, their eyes round and hopeful. "Can we have one, Lizzie? Please?" Annie said.

"Ja, I think that would be all right. But be sure to say thank you," Lizzie said.

The girls hurried toward the door and Dr. McGann accompanied them out of the room. "I'll bring them right back," he called over his shoulder.

"Thank you." Lizzie smiled her gratitude, then faced her father, grateful to have a few moments alone with him.

She moved in close to his bed and took his hand. He squeezed her fingers affectionately.

"How are you doing, really?" he asked.

She released a pensive sigh. *"Gut.* All is well, *vadder.* You needn't worry."

She quickly told him that the bishop had asked Eli

to work their farm and all that the Stoltzfus *familye* had done for them.

"*Ja*, Bishop Yoder came to see me. He thinks having Eli work at the farm is the best thing for us right now."

"Eli and his *familye* have all been very kind."

Jeremiah listened quietly, his brows furrowed in a subtle frown. "I'm grateful to them, but I'm worried too."

"About what?"

He met her gaze, his expression austere. "You. Eli was always much too ambitious and prideful. He wants too much of the world. Don't forget that he left us once. He could do so again. Be wary of him."

Hearing these words, a dark foreboding settled over Lizzie.

"But he's returned now. He says he wants to stay this time. He's even taking the baptism lessons." She didn't know why she defended Eli, but it seemed an automatic response.

"I hope he does stay. But I've seen this happen before. Once members of our faith leave the first time, it's easier to leave a second and third time. Just be careful. I don't want to lose you or see you get hurt again, Elizabeth."

Elizabeth. That alone told her that her father was quite serious. With good reason. Lizzie agreed that her father's concerns were legitimate, but his words sounded too much like Marva Geingerich's. Lizzie couldn't help thinking that everyone deserved a fair, ungrudging second chance. Even Eli. Of course, that didn't mean she loved him and wanted to marry him now. Both of them had grown far apart over the past four years. But she did hope that he found happiness and peace in service to the Lord.

"Has Eli raked the hay yet?" Jeremiah asked.

Lizzie nodded, relieved to change the topic. "He raked it just this morning, before we came into town. Even Deacon Albrecht complimented his work."

Jeremiah nodded. "*Gut.* I'm glad Eli hasn't forgotten how to farm."

They talked for several minutes more, then the girls returned with red-and-green lollipops. They stuck out their tongues, to show how they'd changed colors and they all laughed.

Remembering that Eli had to meet the bishop, Lizzie kept their visit short. They kissed their father goodbye, then walked out into the hall. Eli stood leaning against the wall, holding his black felt hat, his ankles crossed as he stared at the floor. When Lizzie and the girls appeared, he stood up fast, his brows drawn together in a thoughtful frown. Lizzie couldn't help wondering how long he'd been standing there and if he'd overheard her conversation with her father.

"Are you ready to go?" he asked, his voice subdued as he put his hat on his head.

"Ja, danke." She headed toward the outer door.

The two girls skipped along happily beside her as they licked their lollipops.

As always, Eli helped them into the buggy before walking around to the other side. Once they were all settled, he released the brake and called to the horse. As they lurched forward, they each seemed lost in their own thoughts. For the first time since the accident, the girls seemed comfortable riding in a buggy. They finally dozed off, a compliment to Eli and his safe driving. Lizzie felt drowsy too, but couldn't let down her guard enough to sleep. She wasn't really worried they might get hit by another car, but rather she couldn't stop thinking about what her father had said.

Be wary of Eli. It's easier to leave a second and third time.

Would Eli stay or go? Lizzie would never know for certain. Which was exactly why she intended to keep her distance from him.

Chapter Five

As planned, Lizzie and Eli baled hay the following morning, just as soon as the sun had evaporated the glistening dew from the earth. Standing on the baler, she tugged hard on the leather leads to turn the six-hitch team to the right.

"Gee!" she called.

The wagon lurched as the horses stepped forward. The baler trembled. Lizzie widened her stance on the platform to keep from tumbling over the thin railing onto the hard-packed earth.

She was thankful for Tubs and Chubs. As the two strongest horses, Lizzie had hitched them in the middle, providing an anchor and stability to the other four Percherons. The powerful animals leaned into their collars and plodded along without complaint. The soft jingle of their harness mingled with the dull thuds of their heavy hooves as they pulled the baler and hay wagon behind them.

The rattling hum of the gas-powered engine filled Lizzie's ears. The smell of freshly mowed hay was mingled with dust and chaff. She inhaled a slow breath and promptly sneezed. As she reached with one hand for the tissue she kept tucked inside the waist of her black apron, her hip bumped against the guardrail. Not a lot of protection, but it helped steady her on the baler.

She looked over her shoulder. With his legs planted firmly beneath him, Eli swayed easily on the flatbed hay wagon. Taking advantage of the brief lull while they turned the corner, he'd popped up the spout of a blue jug and drank deeply. Water droplets ran down his chin and corded throat before he wiped them away with the back of his hand. As he closed the spout, he looked up and met her gaze. She spun around, embarrassed to be caught staring. But honestly, she just couldn't help herself.

Straightening the horses out to pick up the cut alfalfa, she looked back at the baler. It started up again, churning and spitting out tidy square bales tied together with two strands of heavy twine. She stole a quick glance at Eli again, noticing how he pulled each bundle with ease, the muscles in his shoulders and arms flexing as he tossed the hefty bales onto the quickly expanding stack behind him.

Down one row and up the next, the hay bales piled up and soon filled the wagon. Only a few more rows to go and the hay would be in. No more worries about storm clouds. No more fears of not having the necessary feed for their livestock when the winter snows came deep and cold. No more fretting over…

"Ready to halt!" Eli called above the rumbling of the engine.

"Whoa!" Caught off guard, Lizzie tugged on the leads and the solid horses came to a smooth stop. They seemed unconcerned by this brief interlude, their docked tails swishing back and forth.

The baler and wagon jerked slightly and she looked back to make sure Eli was all right. He had no railing to keep him from falling off the wagon. If he couldn't keep up with the baler, it was her job to slow the horses. But Eli never seemed to have any problems and she couldn't believe how easily he had stepped back into the role of a farmer. If not for the constant ache in her heart, she could almost pretend that he'd never left at all.

He jumped down from the wagon and sauntered over to turn off the baler. "*Ach*, we've done fine work today. Another couple of hours and we'll be finished with the baling."

He flashed a dazzling smile that made his dark eyes sparkle and showed a dimple in his left cheek. Lizzie blinked and turned away, ignoring the swirl of butterflies in her stomach. She was not going to renew her feelings for this man. No, she was not.

She breathed steadily, trying to settle her nerves and enjoying the quiet break for a few moments. By nightfall, they'd be finished with the baling and she could relax. Almost. She wished she had a quiet heart, but worries about her father and all the work still needing to be done weighed heavily on her mind...not to mention her riotous feelings about Eli. In spite of her upbringing and learning to maintain a constant trust in the Lord, her mind felt burdened by doubts. Of course, she would never confess any of that out loud. She didn't want to worry her father or the bishop...or anyone else in the *Gmay*. She must have faith. All would be well. The Lord would care for them. Wouldn't He?

Eli hopped up onto the platform, standing shoulder-to-shoulder with her. She tried not to notice the warmth of his tall frame against her side, but found herself scrunching her arms so she didn't have to feel his sleeve brushing against her.

"May I?" he asked, reaching in front of her to take the lead lines.

She didn't argue as she handed them over. He flashed another smile and her heart gave an odd little thump.

"Schritt!" he called, slapping the leathers lightly against the horses' rumps.

The Percherons stepped forward and the baler gave a sudden wobble. Gripping the guardrail, Lizzie held on with whitened knuckles until they were moving at an even pace. For several moments, she stared at Eli's hands. His fingers were long, graceful and steady, the kind a surgeon would have in a medical office.

Mentally shaking herself, she adjusted the kerchief tied around her head. Because of their grimy work, she'd left her delicate prayer *kapp* in her room earlier that morning.

Within minutes, Eli pulled the horses up in front of the barn. He'd already opened the double doors in the top of the loft and the gas-powered hay elevator sat waiting for them. Marty and Annie came running from the house, but knew to stay out of the way. They watched from a safe distance, sitting on the rail fence in the shade by one of the corrals.

Looping the lead lines over the guardrail, Eli hopped off the baler platform. Lizzie went to join him, but was returning Annie's wave and not paying attention. She lost her balance and felt herself fall. Reaching out, her hands clasped at something, anything to break her fall.

"Oof!" She gasped as she dropped right into Eli's outstretched arms.

She felt the solid wall of his chest against her cheek and heard his steady heartbeat in her ear. Her legs were twisted and she struggled for a moment to regain her footing.

"Are you all right?" he asked, the sound of his deep voice echoing through her entire body.

"I... *ja*, I'm fine."

She looked up and found his face no more than a breath away. Her gaze locked with his and she felt held there by a force she didn't understand. Nothing else existed but them.

Gradually, the farm sounds invaded her dazed brain. The mooing of a cow, the cluck of chickens scratching in the yard. She became aware of the horses and her sisters watching with avid interest. She was also highly conscious of Eli's solid arms clasped around her in a most improper display.

"Are you okay?" Marty called.

"*Ja*, I just lost my balance, that's all."

Lizzie pulled away from Eli and readjusted her apron and kerchief, trying to gather her composure. Trying to pretend she wasn't shocked to discover that she was still highly attracted to this man she could neither forgive nor forget.

Eli stepped back, but she caught the glint of hesitation in his eyes. His startled expression told her that he'd felt the physical attraction between them too. So. He wasn't as unaffected as he portrayed. Which gave her even more reason to keep her distance from him.

Turning aside, he tightened his leather gloves on his finger, then moved over to the hay elevator and started it up. The rattling sound jangled Lizzie's nerves even more. She longed to run to the house and seek sanctuary in her room until her body stopped quaking. But she couldn't leave. There was still work to be done.

That's when she realized why she was in such a foul mood. For some reason, she couldn't bring herself to remain detached from Eli. She told herself it was simply because of what they'd once meant to each other, but somehow she knew it was something more. Something she was having difficulty fighting. And she couldn't help thinking it would be a very long autumn working beside Eli until her father recuperated.

The following morning, Eli scooted the three-legged stool closer to the black-and-white Holstein and sat down. Hunching forward, he applied disinfectant, then set a sterilized silver bucket beneath the cow. With firm squeezes of his fingers, he shot darts of smooth white milk into the bucket. He soon set up an easy rhythm, the metallic whooshing sounds of milk hitting the pail easing the tension in his mind.

Lizzie sat adjacent to him, milking another cow. Marty and Annie were nearby, waiting to assist with pouring the full buckets into the tall canisters. Eli kind of enjoyed the little girls' incessant chatter and spurts of giggles. In the coziness of the barn, it was almost a tranquil moment, except that Lizzie had barely said two words to him.

"Meowwww."

The lazy call of a gray barn cat drew his attention. Without changing his pace, Eli glanced over as the feline slinked its way into the barn. It moved languidly before sidling up against Eli's legs and rubbing its furry head against him in a cajoling manner. When Eli didn't acknowledge the cat, the feline lifted a paw and clawed several times at the hem of his broadfall pants.

Eli chuckled. "Look here, *maed*. Milo is trying to sweet-talk me into giving him some milk."

"Shoo, Milo! This milk isn't for you." Marty rushed at the cat, clapping her hands loudly.

Milo darted over to Lizzie, who had paused long enough to look up. She spared the cat barely a glance before returning to her milking. Milo stayed close by, watching them intently with green eyes.

Luna, a yellow tabby cat, came quickly into the barn with her tail high in the air. She nudged Milo, who greeted her by swatting at her face. Obviously, he didn't want competition in his quest for milk.

Undeterred, Luna sat close by, licking her chops and giving a disgruntled *yowl*. Both cats eyed the milk greedily. Eli smiled, but continued with his work. It soon became difficult to ignore the impatient squalls and growling coming from deep in the back of Milo's throat.

"Meow!"

"What a mournful cry. So pathetic. You'd think they were starving." Lizzie spoke without looking up.

"*Ach*, go away, Luna. You too, Milo. Scat, both of you!" Little Annie copied her sister by clapping her hands, but the felines barely spared the child a glance.

Neither cat was prepared to budge. When both animals started crying repeatedly, Eli finally took pity on them. With perfect aim, he shot a stream of milk, striking Milo directly in the face. The cat sat up on his hind legs and lapped milk off his whiskers. Eli was soon shooting jets of milk into both cats' mouths, one after the other.

Annie squealed with glee. "Look what Eli's doing."

Marty laughed openly at the sight. "How do you do that?"

Eli paused in feeding the two cats and noticed that Lizzie had stopped her milking and was watching him quietly.

"I've had a lot of practice over the years. Doesn't your *vadder* spray milk at the cats?" Eli asked.

"*Ne*, he doesn't," Annie said.

"He'd probably say it was a waste of good milk," Marty said.

Eli shrugged as he shot another gush at the felines, catching them perfectly in the mouth. "The cats have to eat too."

"But they eat mice. That's their job and why they live out here in the barn," Marty said, placing one hand on her hip in a perfect mimic of Lizzie.

Eli laughed out loud. Both children glanced at Lizzie, as if seeking her opinion on the subject.

Lizzie blinked for a couple of moments, then showed a half smile. "It won't do any harm. Milo and Luna won't take enough milk to keep us from making our cheese and cream. And Eli is right. They have to eat too."

Eli was relieved. Though he knew she didn't approve of him, he didn't want to antagonize Lizzie.

He offered a bit more milk. The cats held their front paws aloft and greedily lapped up the treasure. The liquid dripped down the fronts of both animals and dampened their fur, but they didn't seem to mind. One shot caught Milo on the side of his face. He shook his head and made a funny expression before using his paws to wipe and lick off the milk.

Lizzie chuckled out loud. "I think Milo may have had too much already."

Her bright laughter caught Eli off guard. It did something to him inside…a reminder of what they'd once meant to each other and how much he'd loved her. But that was when they were little more than children. He hesitated, feeling mesmerized by her quiet beauty. Loose wisps of hair had come undone from beneath her prayer *kapp* and framed her delicate face. Her blue eyes danced with amusement, her soft lips curved in a smile.

This was the Lizzie he remembered from his childhood. This was the Lizzie he'd fallen in love with all those years earlier. And for just a moment, it was as if he'd never left. She was his Lizzie-bee, who laughed easily and had a warm sense of humor that exposed her intelligence and kindness. He couldn't help thinking of Shannon, who rarely laughed, but had a dry wit that could leave him in stitches. With her short chestnut curls and heavy features, she was so different from Lizzie. And yet, he'd loved them both at separate times in his life. But his feelings for Shannon had been more mature. More lasting. His love for Lizzie had been only a childish infatuation. Hadn't it?

"Do it again, Eli. Do it again," Annie encouraged.

Awakened from his mindless wandering, Eli took careful aim and shot more milk at the cats. When Luna started licking Milo's furry coat, they all laughed. Eli's attention was drawn to Lizzie's beaming face again. Her eyes were bright, her expression vibrant as she watched the barn cats' funny antics. She glanced up and her gaze locked with his. Then, she frowned, as if she'd remembered all the sadness that still lay between them.

"*Ach*, I think that's enough. We need to get back to work." Lizzie turned on her stool and returned to her milking.

Eli did likewise, noticing that the two cats had started licking themselves to clean every drop of milk off their fur.

Marty and Annie didn't complain as he handed off his filled milk pail to them. He waited patiently as the girls carried it over to the tall container, lifted it and poured the contents in. While they were occupied with that chore, he glanced over at Lizzie and found her watching him. She jerked, looking embarrassed. Her bucket was also full and she hesitated, not seeming to know what to do with herself until the girls returned for her milk.

"It's good to hear you laugh again," Eli spoke low.

She swallowed and looked down at her shoes. "I laugh all the time."

No, she didn't. Not anymore. Not the deep, hearty laughter that exposed the joy she felt inside. In fact, the absence of her laughter was very telling. Very rarely did her eyes sparkle, or her lips curve up with amusement. Eli knew she wasn't happy. Not anymore. And he wasn't certain if it was because of him or because of the added responsibilities resting on her slender shoulders.

Maybe both.

"You used to laugh all the time," he said. "Remem-

ber when we went fishing together? We had a lot of
fun then."

Her frown deepened. "That was a long time ago."

"It's just been four short years."

"It's been four long years," she said.

She looked away, her expression wistful and sad. He
didn't need to ask why. It had been only four years, and
yet it had been a lifetime. But more than that, his reminder had crushed the tenuous humor between them.
Even the two cats frolicking in the hay couldn't get a
smile out of Lizzie now.

Marty returned with his empty bucket and he
ducked his head, resuming his milking. Out of his
peripheral vision, he watched as the little girls emptied Lizzie's bucket and she moved on to the next cow.
He longed to chat about inconsequential things as he
worked, but didn't know what to say anymore. Lizzie
seemed to feel the same way. She was overly quiet,
as if she wished she were with anyone but him. They
used to be so comfortable with each other. So natural and relaxed. Their discussions and laughter were
spontaneous. And he felt suddenly very sorry that he
and Lizzie had lost the camaraderie between them.

While the girls remained behind to feed the pigs
and collect eggs, Lizzie finished her chores, then hurried to the house. Watching her go, Eli felt an emptiness inside his chest. It reminded him of how alone
he really was and he missed Shannon more than ever
before. His ruined relationship with Lizzie seemed to
make his solitude even worse.

Chapter Six

A number of days later, Lizzie shook out a damp sheet and hung it over the clothesline. She quickly attached it at each end and put a couple of pins in the middle, to keep it from sagging to the ground. In spite of the chill in the air, morning sunlight gleamed across the yard, a mild breeze coming from the east. Red, gold and brown leaves fluttered to the ground. Maybe later that afternoon, she could get the girls to rake the front yard.

By noon, the laundry should be dry and ready to be ironed and put away. She took a deep inhale, enjoying the momentarily peaceful interlude and the beauty of the autumn leaves. Once the weather turned, she'd have to hang their clothes on racks inside the house to dry.

The rattle of a buggy caught her attention and she lifted her head toward the dirt road. Mervin Schwartz pulled into the front yard. Wiping her hands on her apron, Lizzie went to greet him. She held the horse steady while Mervin heaved himself off the buggy seat. A portly man of perhaps forty-five years, he winced as he tried to step down.

"Let me help you." Lizzie took his arm, noticing he wore a work boot on his right foot and only a heavy wool sock on his left.

"Danke," he spoke in a breathless wheeze once he stood on the ground. He favored the shoeless foot as he hobbled toward the front porch.

"Do you have an injury?" she asked, helping him climb the steps to the front door. Instead of going inside, he dropped down into one of the low Adirondack chairs *Daed* had made with his own hands.

"Ne, but I've got the gout something terrible." He groaned, easing himself back as he gripped the armrests of the chair.

"I'm so sorry. What can I do? Can I get you something?" she asked, feeling a bit helpless and wondering why he'd come all the way out here to their farm when he should be home, resting.

Mervin shook his head, his face flushed with sweat in spite of the cool day. "I came to see Eli Stoltzfus. He helped Deacon Albrecht with his leg wound and I'm hoping he'll know what I can do to ease the pain in my foot."

Lizzie blinked, thinking Mervin had lost his mind. "But Eli isn't a doctor."

"I don't want a doctor. Eli is one of us and yet he's had schooling and will know what to do for me."

His obvious faith in Eli astonished Lizzie. A number of her people served one another according to their specialties. Amos Yoder was the best blacksmith in their community. Linda Hostetler dried plants to make special teas, ointments, tonics, salves and liniments.

Everyone valued their contributions. But their skills had been learned at home, as part of the community. Not through a fancy education in the *Englisch* world. To have a member of their congregation ask for Eli's help specifically because he'd received a college education seemed odd to Lizzie, especially since her people shunned higher learning.

"I… I'll see if I can find Eli," she said.

Stepping down from the porch, she rounded the house and hurried toward the barn. Inside, the musty scent of clean straw filled her nose as she blinked to let her eyes become accustomed to the dim interior. Eli sat on the top of an old barrel, a harness spread across his lap as he mended the leather straps. Lizzie wasn't surprised to find Marty and Annie helping him. The girls both liked Eli and he was kind to them. Wherever he was, they were usually there too. Just now, her sisters were pulling the lead lines out of the way, holding them straight so he could make sense of the melee of straps, hooks and buckles.

"*Ach*, that's good. Hold it steady now."

Eli bent his dark head over the mess, his long, graceful fingers pulling apart a particularly stubborn knot. His black felt hat hung from a hook on the wall, his short hair curling against the nape of his neck.

In the quiet of the barn, no one seemed to notice Lizzie. For a few moments, she stood watching from the shadows, enjoying the serenity of the scene. Then, she cleared her throat.

"Eli?"

He looked up, his handsome mouth curved in a ready smile, his sharp gaze seeming to nail her to the wall.

"Lizzie-bee." He said her name softly, like a caress, and she couldn't help shivering.

She folded her arms. "Um, Mervin Schwartz is up at the house. He's hoping you can help him with his gout."

Eli's forehead crinkled as he stood and laid the harness on the ground before looking at the little girls. "Well then, my two good assistants, it seems we will have to mend the harness later on. Right now, someone needs our help."

He smiled and tugged playfully on the ribbons of their prayer *kapps* before whisking his hat off the hook and heading toward Lizzie. He paused at the door, pushing it wide while he waited for her to precede him outside. She did so, feeling suddenly flustered by his good manners. The little girls exited as well, and then raced ahead of them. As Lizzie walked toward the house, she was more than conscious of Eli following behind. She could almost feel his steely eyes boring a hole in her back.

The girls greeted Mervin and initially watched with curiosity as the two men discussed the problem, but the girls soon disappeared when Mervin removed his sock and revealed a rather hairy foot with a large, red bump on the side of his big toe. Even Lizzie could tell it was inflamed. The skin looked red and dry, with an odor like Limburger cheese emanating from his toes. Trying to hide her grimace, Lizzie stood back, feeling a bit repulsed. But not Eli.

With infinite gentleness, he knelt before Mervin and cupped the front of the man's foot in both hands. When Eli lightly touched the bump with his fingertips, Mervin inhaled a sharp breath through his teeth.

"It hurts, huh?" Eli asked without looking up.

"*Ja*, a lot. I can hardly stand to walk on it and I've got chores needing to be done. Can you do something to help me?" Mervin asked.

Lizzie could hardly believe Eli didn't draw back in disgust. A vision of the Savior washing the feet of His disciples suddenly flashed inside her mind and she couldn't help respecting Eli for not shying away.

Looking up, Eli met Lizzie's gaze. "Do you have a bag of frozen peas and a clean dish towel I can use?"

She nodded, thinking of all the foods they had stuffed inside their propane-powered refrigerator. She wasn't naive enough to ask why he needed the peas.

Whirling around, she hurried inside and opened the small freezer box. She rummaged around until she found what she was after, snapped up a dish towel, then raced back outside.

The screen door clapped closed behind her as she handed the items to Eli. After scooting another chair close in front of Mervin, Eli wrapped the cloth around the bag of frozen peas. With gentle precision, he lifted Mervin's foot to the chair and laid the cold compress across his big toe.

Mervin laid his head back and groaned, closing his eyes for several moments.

Sitting next to Mervin, Eli met his gaze. "You know I'm not a doctor, right?"

"*Ja*, but you know what I need, don't you?" Mervin responded in a half-desperate voice.

"*Ja*, you need a qualified doctor," Eli said. "Someone like Dr. McGann can prescribe some medicine to help reduce the uric acid in your joints. All I can suggest is that you take an anti-inflammatory medication, drink lots of water and eat a handful of cherries every day."

Mervin blinked, taking in every word. "Cherries?"

"*Ja*, they're a natural way to reduce the uric acid. But a doctor can give you a complete list of other foods to eat or avoid eating."

Tilting his head to one side, Mervin's jowls bobbed. "Like what kinds of foods to avoid?"

Eli shrugged. "Things like bacon, fish, liver, beef, corn syrup..."

Mervin's eyes widened. "Liver? Bacon?"

"*Ja*, they're high in purine, which contributes to the uric acid in your blood. They'll make the gout worse."

"*Ach!*" Mervin lifted a hand to his face as he shook his head. "I eat liver almost every morning. I love it covered with fried onions."

"I'd recommend you no longer eat it. I'd also recommend you lose twenty pounds."

Mervin frowned.

Eli rested a consoling hand on the man's arm. "You may need to give up a few foods and watch your portion sizes, but I guarantee it'll help you feel better. But more than anything, it's important for you to go see Dr. McGann as soon as possible."

Mervin pursed his lips, his face slightly flushed with repugnance. "But he's an *Englischer*."

He said it as if it were a dirty word. Although they all lived among the *Englisch* and did business with them, some of their people didn't like to mingle with them any more than absolutely necessary.

"*Ja*, Dr. McGann is *Englisch*. But he's also experienced, capable and kind. He won't force you to do what you don't want to do, but he can ease a lot of your pain. Go see him. I wouldn't send you to him if I didn't believe he could help."

A deep frown settled across Mervin's forehead. "All right. I'll go. But only because you trust him."

"I do. Explicitly," Eli said.

His concession seemed to ease the tension in Mervin's shoulders. Lizzie quickly made a pitcher of lemonade for them to enjoy and they talked about inconsequential things for a short time. When Eli removed the bag of peas, Mervin announced that his big toe felt a bit better.

"It's just a dull throb. I believe I can even stand the drive home now," Mervin said with delight.

"Good. But I fear it won't last long. The pain will return," Eli said.

"That's all right. I'll go see Doc McGann tomorrow and buy some cherries at the grocery store on my way home. And I'll ask Hannah to fix something else for breakfast besides fried liver."

Eli chuckled and Lizzie couldn't help smiling too. They assisted the man to his buggy and she couldn't help noticing Eli's caring compassion. He ensured the man was seated comfortably before handing him the lead lines.

"You drive safely. And I'll check back with you at church on Sunday," Eli said.

"*Danke*. You've been a lot of help, my friend. It's *gut* to have you back home where you belong." Mervin tipped his hat, then clicked to the horse.

As the buggy pulled away, Lizzie couldn't help shooting a sideways glance at Eli. She studied him for just a moment, then flinched when he turned abruptly and caught her watching him.

"*Ach*, look how the time has flown," she said. "I've still got so much work to do. I shouldn't have visited so long."

Turning, she hurried toward the house, trying to ignore the weight of his gaze following her. Her brain churned with confusion. Though she disapproved of Eli's worldly knowledge, she could see how it could benefit their people. That was good, wasn't it? But such knowledge often led to *Hochmut*. And pride was never a good thing. It kept a person from being humble and receptive to *Gott*'s will. And the fact that Eli had gotten his education prior to committing to their faith seemed a bit like cheating to Lizzie. He'd known all along that he could make peace with his people as long as he got his education before being baptized. It seemed he'd gotten what he wanted from the *Englisch* world, which meant it likely cost him little to return. So, how could she accept Eli and his higher learning now? She couldn't. It was that simple.

An hour after Mervin left, Eli had finished repairing the harness and taken Billie out for a drive with the buggy. He wanted to see if the horse was skittish around passing cars and trucks. He was delighted when the animal didn't even flinch.

Now, Eli stood at the side of the barn chopping wood. Wielding an ax, he split the last piece of kindling, then sank the blade of the tool into the top of the chopping block. Arching his back, Eli wiped his forehead with his shirtsleeve, thinking he'd have this cord of wood split by the middle of next week. As he eyed the neatly stacked pile of kindling, he felt satisfied that the Beilers wouldn't run out of fuel for their cookstove this winter.

"Oh, no you don't. Get out of here. Shoo!"

Eli jerked around, wondering what had caused such a frenzy of shouts. Wielding a broom, Lizzie chased two fat pigs across the backyard. Her laundry basket sat on its side beneath the clothesline. Obviously, she had dropped it there when she came out to collect the laundry…and found pigs in the yard. One of the swine raced toward the garden just beyond the clothesline.

"Ne!" Lizzie tore after the animal, swatting its hindquarters with the broom.

The pig squealed and veered right, barely missing the clean sheet. Understanding how the animals could ruin Lizzie's hard work if they tangled with the laundry, Eli raced forward to help her.

"Haw! Haw!" he yelled, waving his arms to direct the swine back toward their pen.

The pigs snorted and oinked as they pattered in the right direction, their short legs moving fast.

Flanking them on the right, Lizzie helped Eli herd them into the pen.

Victory!

Before the animals could escape again, Eli shut the gate. In the process, his boots slipped in the mud and down he went, landing on his backside.

Lizzie gasped. "Eli! Are you hurt?"

Standing just inside the gate, she gripped her broom like a savage warrior. She looked so fierce and endearing that he couldn't contain a chuckle.

Sitting in the mud, he bit his tongue. The cold muck seeped through his pants, soaking him to the skin. Lifting his hands, he flung great dollops of black sludge off his fingers. Now what would he do? He had an afternoon of chores left to complete with no clean change of clothes.

A chortling sound caused him to look up. Lizzie stood in front of him, trying—and failing—to hide her laughter behind her hand.

Eli tilted his head. "May I ask what is so funny?"

She hunched her shoulders, no longer laughing, but her smile stayed firmly in place. "You are. I think you are a bit too old to play in the *dreck*."

He looked down at himself, noting how long it would take to get the mud off, then looked back at her. "*Ja*, I agree. When you can quit laughing, would you mind helping me up?"

He held out his arm and waited. Leaning her broom against the pen, she took firm hold of his hand, braced her feet and pulled hard.

A heavy sucking sound heralded his freedom from the mud. As he stood before her, he felt absolutely dismayed by his predicament...until he heard her laughter again. When he glanced up, her laughter cut off, but her eyes twinkled with mirth. Being near her made his heart rate trip into double time. In spite of her frequent looks of disapproval, he felt happy being around her and figured it must be because they'd been so close once.

"You have *dreck* on your face." He reached his free hand up to wipe a streak of mud off the tip of her nose.

She gave an embarrassed giggle. "At least I'm not wearing it all over my clothes."

He chuckled helplessly and indicated her nose. "I'm sorry, but I just made it worse."

She wiped at her face, removing most of the muck.

Looking into her sparkling blue eyes, he felt thoroughly enchanted. She stared back at him, her lips slightly parted. Then he remembered that Shannon's eyes were a dark amber color and his heart gave a painful squeeze.

He stepped back, feeling flushed with shame. It was disloyal for him to flirt with another woman, wasn't it? Shannon was gone, but his heart was still tied to her. He couldn't seem to let go of the pain or the guilt. It was on the tip of his tongue to tell Lizzie about his fiancée. To confide his heartache over Shannon's death. But Lizzie's expression changed to a doubtful scowl.

She turned toward the house. "I'd better get the laundry gathered in and finish making sandwiches. I'll lay out some of *Daed*'s clothing on the back porch if you'd like to get cleaned up. Then you can join us for lunch."

Without waiting for his reply, she walked fast toward the clothesline. He watched as she rinsed her hands with the garden hose, then jerked the pins from the clean sheets and haphazardly folded them and the other clothing before dropping each piece into the laundry basket. Without a backward glance, she went inside. Only when the door closed behind her did he realize he was still staring.

Swallowing heavily, he shivered as a cool breeze swept over him. He headed toward the house, eager to get out of his damp clothes. When he'd stared into Lizzie's eyes, he'd felt the attraction between them. But it wasn't right. Shannon should be here with him, not Lizzie. He'd been Shannon's fiancé and would have soon been her husband. It had been his job to look after her, to protect her, but he'd failed miserably. And it occurred to him that he'd failed Lizzie too. Twice, he'd lost the opportunity to marry the woman he loved. And both times, it had been his own fault. Though he longed to have a *familye* of his own, maybe he'd let the chance for happiness pass him by.

Pushing his morose thoughts aside, he went to the outside faucet and rinsed himself off. He gasped and trembled in the frigid water. After he'd rinsed the muck off his work boots, he stepped up onto the back porch in his bare feet and found a pile of clean clothing waiting for him along with a fluffy towel. He quickly retired to the barn where he got cleaned up. When he returned to the kitchen, Marty and Annie were already seated at the table. The spicy aroma of allspice and cloves filled his senses.

"We waited for you, Eli. Lizzie made pumpkin bread," little Annie chirped in a happy tone.

"First, you must eat a sandwich." Lizzie stood in front of the counter, slicing homemade bread. She didn't spare him a glance as she set a plate of bologna and cheese on the table beside a bowl of sliced melon.

"We're real hungry and you took a long time," Marty added, her forehead creased with impatience.

He smiled, noticing that Annie's *kapp* was crooked. As he took his seat, he straightened it, then brushed his finger against the tip of her nose. "*Ach*, I'm famished too. Let's eat."

Once Lizzie sat down, they each bowed their head for a silent prayer. After a few moments, Eli breathed a quiet sigh and they all dug in.

"Lizzie says she's gonna cook a turkey for Thanksgiving," Marty said.

"But I want ham," Annie said. She swiveled around to look at Eli. "What's your favorite? Ham or turkey?"

He hesitated before answering truthfully. "I think I prefer stuffed turkey for Thanksgiving and ham for Christmas dinner. Now, what's your favorite pie?"

Annie tilted her head and looked up at the ceiling, as if contemplating this deep subject. "Hmm, I think I like pumpkin the best. But Lizzie always makes pecan and apple too."

"Yum! I'd like a giant slice of each kind," Annie said.

Eli chuckled, enjoying this light conversation. If not for Lizzie being overly quiet, he would have felt completely relaxed. He had to remind himself that this wasn't his *familye* and his visit here was temporary. "That's a lot of pie for such a little *maedel*. Are you sure you can eat all of that?"

"Sure I can. I could eat it all day long." Annie nodded as she took a big bite of her sandwich to make her point.

"How come you left and didn't marry Lizzie?" Marty asked the question so abruptly that Eli choked on a bite of buttered bread. He coughed to clear his throat and took several deep swallows from his glass of chilled milk.

"Didn't you love her no more?" Annie asked before he could reply.

"Anymore," Lizzie corrected in a stern voice. "And it's none of your business."

"Well," Eli began, speaking slowly so he could gather his scattered thoughts. "We were both very young at the time and I wanted to know more about the world before I committed to our faith and settled down to raise a *familye*."

There, that was good. He'd rehearsed the explanation more than once, not wanting to admit that he'd been too frightened to marry so young. He'd wanted to go to school instead. To see and learn more about this world he lived in before he settled down for the rest of his life.

He was about to enlarge on his explanation when Lizzie set her fork down and rose slowly to her feet. Her eyes were narrowed and flashed with an emotion he couldn't name…a mixture of despair and anger.

When she spoke, her voice sounded hoarse with suppressed emotion. "It would have been nice if you had explained all of that to me instead of disappearing without a single word."

Eli stared at her, his mind a riot of thoughts he didn't know how to express. How could she say he hadn't explained? He'd told her everything in his letters. Why hadn't she replied? Why had she ignored his efforts to reach out to her? She could have written back to him.

Before he could think of a satisfactory response, Lizzie walked out to the backyard, pulling the door closed quietly behind her.

The little girls stared after their sister, their gazes round with uncertainty.

"Is Lizzie mad at us?" Annie's lip quivered, her eyes welling up with tears.

"*Ne*, she's not angry at you. Please don't cry." Eli set his sandwich on his plate.

Lizzie wasn't mad at her sisters. She was mad at him.

"I'll go check on her and see if I can get her to come back inside." He stood and smiled, speaking in a light tone he hoped would soothe them. "You two finish your lunch and I'll smooth everything over. Okay?"

They both nodded. He went outside, wondering if he should simply take his muddy clothes and go home. It had been a difficult day and he wasn't sure what to expect when he found Lizzie.

She stood leaning against the tool shed, staring out at the stubbled fields. Tomorrow, he planned to harrow and smooth out the small ruts in preparation for spring planting. When he approached, she quickly wiped her eyes. *Ach*, did she have to cry?

"Lizzie?" He spoke gently, not sure what to say. He didn't want to create more friction between them.

She faced him, her eyes damp and filled with such misery that it nearly broke his heart.

"Why did you have to go away to school? And why are so many people asking for your help?" she asked.

Taken off guard by her questions, he shrugged. "You know why I went to school. And I suppose people come to me because they think I can make their ailments better."

"Can't you stop it?"

"Would you rather I sent them away?"

She looked down at her feet. "*Ne*, that wouldn't be right. You have to help them if you can."

"I don't *have* to help them, but I *want* to, Lizzie. I believe it's what the Savior would have me to do."

"*Ja*, you're right. It's just that…just that…"

She didn't finish her statement, but she didn't have to. Finally they were getting at the crux of the problem.

"It's the fact that I went to college that bothers you,

isn't it? That I lived among the *Englisch* and became a paramedic. Right?"

She nodded. "On the one hand, your skills are so beneficial. But on the other hand, it was wrong for you to leave. Higher learning can cause too much *Hochmut*."

"Is that what you think? That I'm filled with pride?"

"*Ja, ne… Ach*, I don't know anymore. When you left so suddenly, I didn't know what to think. I can't even tell you how badly you hurt me. I thought we were going to marry."

He sighed and looked away. "We were too young, Lizzie. At the time, I truly loved you. But we both needed time to become adults. You know that."

Her mouth dropped open. "So you just forgot about your promises to me? You didn't even have the common courtesy to say goodbye."

Confusion fogged his brain. "I… I left you a long letter explaining everything. And I wrote to you many times afterward. Not once did you respond to me."

Her forehead furrowed in bewilderment. "You wrote your *eldre*, Eli. Your *mudder* shared some of your letters with me, but you never wrote directly to me. Not once."

Taking a step closer, he lifted a hand, forcing himself to be slow to anger. His faith had taught him to be a better man than to yell and say things he'd regret later on. His father had also taught him that a soft answer turned away wrath. So, he spoke in a gentle voice, hoping it worked.

"I wrote to you dozens of times, Lizzie. I… I didn't dare say goodbye to anyone in person because I feared you and my *eldre* would stop me from going. It's hard to explain, but I wanted to know more about the world. I couldn't stay. But I am wondering why you never responded to my letters. Why would you pretend they never existed?"

She shook her head, looking miserable. "I never received any letters from you. Not ever."

Doubt clogged his brain. He'd never known her to lie, so why would she do so now? There had to be another explanation.

"I don't know what to say," he said. "I wrote you many times, but every letter was returned unopened. I told you that I loved you and asked you to join me in Denver, but I never heard back from you."

She snorted. "Even if I had received these letters from you, it would have made no difference in my decisions. I would never have abandoned my faith to become an *Englisch* woman."

Though she spoke softly, he caught the contempt in her voice. The disdain. To her, the *Englisch* were worldly and ungodly…everything she didn't want to be.

"I know that now," he said. "But it took a long time for me to realize you would not agree to come to me. After a year, when I didn't hear from you, I finally accepted that I had lost you for good and moved on with my life."

But he didn't tell her about Shannon. If Lizzie knew he'd fallen in love with an *Englisch* girl, it might deepen her disgust for him.

"You moved on without me the moment you left," she said. "You loved worldly pursuits more than you loved me. More than you loved *Gott*. And that is because you had too much *Hochmut*. I don't know what has brought you back home, but it doesn't change anything between us. And now, I have work to do."

Lifting her chin, she brushed past him and headed toward the house, her spine stiff and unapproachable. Watching her go, he couldn't help wondering what had happened to all of his letters. They'd been returned, they were now in his possession, but who had sent them back to him? Perhaps Jeremiah? He didn't know for sure.

It didn't matter. He and Lizzie no longer loved one another. Time had drawn them apart and they'd found other lives and other loves. There could be nothing else between them. Not now, not ever.

Chapter Seven

Lizzie slid a canister of freshly made cheese curd into the chilled water of the well house. Vague sunlight gleamed through the open doorway, the air filled with the pungent scent of rain. Higher up in the mountains, it had snowed last night. Just a light dusting, but enough to lower the temperature substantially.

Brr! Lizzie snuggled deeper into her heavy black coat and tightened the blue hand knitted scarf around her neck. The chores were finished and it was time to go inside for the evening. Eli should be leaving to go home soon. For two days, she'd purposefully avoided him after their last discussion. Tomorrow, they'd pay another visit to *Daed* in town. Maybe the doctor would even let him come home. While they would still need Eli to continue on the farm during *Daed*'s recovery, she'd feel more secure with her father's presence.

Stepping outside, she secured the door, then crossed the yard. She glanced toward the barn, noticing a light gleaming beneath the double doors. Eli was still working. She thought about going to see what was keeping him so late, but decided against it. After all that had happened between them, she needed to keep her distance.

A few days earlier, during Church Sunday, he'd been surrounded by several members of their congregation. They each sought guidance on how to cure their various ailments...everything from a persistent cough to shingles. Eli had insisted he wasn't a doctor, but offered his best advice. He then encouraged each person to go into town and visit Dr. McGann as soon as possible.

"Eli! Eli Stoltzfus!"

Lizzie whirled around and saw David Hostetler driving his horse and buggy at a breakneck speed along the dirt road. Gravel flew into the air as the horse pulled into the main yard. The animal was breathing hard and Lizzie ran to see what was the matter.

In a rush, David jumped out of the buggy, then reached back to lift out his seven-year-old son, Timothy. The boy was wrapped tightly in a quilt with only his face visible. He groaned and Lizzie instantly noticed the child's rasping breath, his eyes fluttering open and closed, and his lips a bluish color.

"What is wrong?" she asked.

"Can I help?" Eli startled her when he reached to press a hand to his forehead. Dressed in his warm winter coat and black felt hat, Eli must have just been preparing to go home when he heard David's cries and came running from the barn.

Standing back, Lizzie gave Eli room as David headed toward the front porch.

"He...he breathed in pesticide. He spilled it down his front," David said, his voice sharp and slightly breathless from his exertions.

"Bring him inside," Eli said, his voice and manner urgent.

Without a backward glance, he opened the door and they hurried into the front room. Lizzie followed, anticipating they might need her help. Eli led David straight through to the kitchen.

Startled by the commotion, Annie and Marty hopped up from the couch where they had been reading by lamplight. Standing barefoot in their warm flannel nightgowns, they gazed at the group with a mixture of alarm and shock.

"Lizzie?" Always sensitive to other people's troubles, Annie took her hand.

Lizzie wrapped one arm around the girl's shoulders and pulled her close. "It's all right, *boppli*. Timmy is sick, but we're going to help him get better."

They followed the men into the kitchen.

"Lay him on the table," Eli ordered.

David did so. The boy moaned, his voice a scratchy gurgle.

Eli glanced her way. "Do you have some rubber gloves I can use?"

She nodded, opened the cupboard door beneath the sink and handed him the items. Eli quickly tugged them on, then pulled the quilt aside. Timmy was still dressed in his work clothes. Lizzie's nose twitched as the heavy odor of pesticide struck her. She crinkled her forehead, understanding why her father rarely used such volatile chemicals on his farm. If they were dangerous to bugs, they were dangerous to humans.

Eli looked up at her. "Lizzie, please have the *maed* leave the room immediately. I don't want anyone to touch Timmy or his clothes except me. Not until we can get the poison off him. The quilt and Timmy's clothes should be burned. I doubt anyone can get them clean enough to use again. Don't handle them except with rubber gloves. I don't want you to get hurt. Do you understand?"

She nodded, realizing the gravity of the situation. But for him to say he didn't want her to get hurt made her heart thud. She told herself it meant nothing. That he was only looking out for her the same as he would do for anyone. But for just a moment, she secretly wished it meant a bit more. Then, she reminded herself that they were barely even friends.

"David needs to wash his hands and arms with soap and hot water. He's been holding Timmy and probably has poison on his skin. Lizzie, you'll need to clean the sink afterward with cleanser. Be sure to wear rubber gloves."

She nodded stoically. Without a word, she ushered her sisters out of the room. David followed, leaving his son in Eli's care.

"But I wanna stay," Marty complained.

Understanding the problem very well, Lizzie didn't back down. Just breathing in pesticides or getting them on the skin could do grave damage. Besides, the girls would only be in the way if they stayed.

"*Ne*, my *liebchen*. The poison could hurt you too. In fact, it's time for you and Annie to go to bed." Taking each girl's hand, Lizzie pulled them along.

"*Ach!* I don't wanna go to bed," Annie whined.

Without a word, Lizzie pointed toward the bathroom and spoke to David. "There are clean towels in the cupboard and plenty of soap by the sink. You can borrow one of *Daed*'s clean shirts too. Remember not to touch anything you don't need to as it will spread the poison."

He nodded and headed that way.

Lizzie walked up the stairs with her sisters. "I'm sorry, but it's time to sleep and I need to help the men with Timmy."

"But what if Timmy di-dies?" Annie's voice trembled.

"No one is going to die. We must trust in *Gott* and Eli is going to do everything he can to help." Lizzie tried to make her voice sound calm and soothing, but her pulse pounded with trepidation. Even she could see that Timmy was having difficulty breathing. He obviously needed serious medical care and she wondered what Eli could do with their limited resources.

"Don't worry," Marty said. "Eli will make Timmy better. He knows what to do."

Her sister's confidence in Eli surprised Lizzie. And in her heart of hearts, she said a silent prayer, hoping her sister was right.

When Lizzie returned to the kitchen a few minutes later, David was just coming out of the bathroom. He rolled the sleeves of one of *Daed*'s shirts down his damp arms as he walked swiftly with her to the kitchen.

"I cleaned everything I touched, so we wouldn't have poison spread around your bathroom," he said.

Eli looked up as they entered the room. He held Timmy's wrist, taking his pulse with his bare hand. As soon as he finished, he pulled the rubber glove back on. "Lizzie, would you fill the bathtub with warm water? Timmy still has poison on him and we've got to wash it all off. He'll need some warm, clean clothes to wear too."

"Of course," she said, racing into the bathroom.

Over the next twenty minutes, they did what they could for Timmy. Lizzie found some fresh though rather large clothes for him to wear. By the time he was cleaned up, his breathing came a little easier, but he still had a dry, hacking cough. Eli doffed the rubber gloves, which he'd washed off. When he handed them to Lizzie, his warm fingers touched hers. She looked up and their eyes met for a few brief moments.

"It'll be all right," he whispered for her ears alone, then turned back to the boy.

Lizzie shivered, trying to ignore how Eli's kind words impacted her. He was worried about Timmy, that was all.

She put on the rubber gloves, then carefully folded Timmy's contaminated clothes inside the quilt. As she carried them outside to burn later on, she turned her face away from the heavy stench of poison.

Back inside, she provided a clean quilt and helped Eli wrap it around the boy to alleviate his trembling.

"Daedi," Timmy called in a weak voice, his eyes closed. In spite of the chill air, he was sweating profusely.

"I'm here, *sohn*." David smoothed his fingers through the boy's slightly damp hair, his big hands trembling.

"I'm sorry. I didn't mean to spill the poison. Are you *bees* at me?"

David gave a laughing scoff, which sounded more like a low sob. *"Ne*, I'm not angry with you. Don't worry, *sohn*. I just want you to get better."

Eli checked the boy's eyes again, then checked his pulse. With pursed lips, he looked at David. "He's breathing better, but not good enough. This *kind* needs a hospital right now. His heart rate is too slow and his pupils are still contracted."

David lifted his hands. "But can't you make him better? I don't want to take him to the hospital if we can avoid it. They're all *Englisch* there and don't understand our ways."

Eli shook his head emphatically. "I've done all I can for him. The hospital has antidotes and respirators to help Timmy. If you want him to live, we need to take him there immediately."

Lizzie hated to admit it, but she thought Eli was right. If they didn't take Timmy to the hospital, he would die. But were it not for Eli, he would be dead already. The quick, capable care Eli provided had eased the symptoms. Hopefully that would be enough to give them time to get Timothy to the hospital. In all these years, she'd condemned Eli for leaving her to seek higher learning. But now, watching him trying to save Timmy's life, she realized his profession was a great benefit.

"What pesticide were you using?" Eli asked.

"Malathion. I sprayed my cornfield, hoping to kill the earworms so I'll have a bigger crop next year. When my back was turned, Timmy tried to mix some of the concentrated poison himself. He was only trying to help, but he spilled it down his shirtfront and breathed in a lot of fumes. I've got the container outside in my buggy."

"*Gut.* That was smart to bring it with you. The hospital will need to know exactly what chemicals we're dealing with. *Komm*, let's go." Taking for granted that

David would follow, Eli picked up Timmy and carried him through to the living room.

Lizzie followed, grasping the handle of a gas lamp and holding it high as David opened the front door and they all stepped out onto the porch. A brisk wind made Lizzie gasp. Night had fallen, the frosty air thick with the promise of snow. At some point during the melee, she'd doffed her warm coat and now wrapped an arm around herself. Darkness shrouded the farm in shadows and she hated to let the men leave without her. Hated not knowing the outcome of this frenzied night. But she would have to remain behind with her sisters.

She held the lamp high as the men climbed into the buggy and settled Timmy comfortably. With a frantic yell, David slapped the lead lines against the horse's back and they took off at a swift trot. Before the buggy turned onto the main road, Eli threw a quick look back at Lizzie. In the vague moonlight, she saw him lift one hand in farewell and mouth the word *danke*. Or at least, she thought that's what he said. She wasn't certain.

She waved, but felt haunted by Eli's gaze. In his eyes, she saw something that she'd never seen there before. Complete and utter fear. But what did it mean? Was he afraid Timmy might die? Or was his fear connected to something else? She had no idea, but sensed it had a deeper meaning than just the possibility of losing Timmy.

Lizzie hurried into the waiting warmth of the house. Thankfully, it wasn't snowing yet. It would normally take thirty precious minutes for the men to make it to the hospital in town…twenty minutes at the swift speed they were traveling. She only hoped and prayed the horse could stand the rapid pace.

* * *

Timmy trembled and Eli tucked the quilt tighter around him. Gazing at the boy's ashen cheeks, Eli feared the worst. A vision of Shannon's pale face filled his mind. Her weak voice as she begged him to save her life chimed in his ears. Her cries of fear as he tried to stop the bleeding seemed to haunt him. Her brown eyes as they closed for the last time never left his mind for long. He'd failed her. He couldn't save her life. And what if he lost Timmy too? He loved being a paramedic. Loved helping others. But he couldn't lose another patient. He just couldn't!

"Can't we go any faster?" he asked.

David slapped the leads hard against the horse's back. The animal plunged onward at a breakneck speed. "I don't dare push Ben any harder for fear he'll collapse and leave us afoot. I'm also worried a car might come up from behind and crash into the back of us."

Of course. What was Eli thinking? This was a horse and buggy, not an automobile. He'd grown too used to the *Englisch* world where he'd ridden everywhere in cars, trucks and buses. The rapid speed had spoiled him for this slower pace. He had to remember that he was in the Amish world now, where he should rely on faith and *Gott*'s will to get them through. Above all else, they needed to arrive safely. It'd do Timmy no good if the horse dropped dead of exhaustion, or if they collided with a car. Then they'd have to carry the boy into town on foot and they might arrive too late.

Minutes passed slowly until they finally crested a hill and the lights of Riverton came into view. A fresh pulse of anxiousness swept over Eli. Just a few more minutes now.

"Timmy, *vie gehts*?" he asked the boy, trying to keep him awake…to ensure he was still alive.

"Uh-huh." The child's voice sounded vague and his eyes barely fluttered.

"We're almost there now. You're doing fine. Soon, you'll be up and running around your farm with your *brieder* and *schweschder*."

Eli spoke to Timmy over and over again, trying to encourage the boy. Trying to encourage himself. He mustn't give up hope. He must exercise faith. And for the first time since Shannon's death, he offered a silent prayer for help.

When David pulled the buggy in front of the small emergency room, no orderly came out to greet them like they did at the large hospital where Eli had worked in Denver. Overhead lights gleamed brightly in the covered driveway with very few cars in the dark parking lot…not surprising in this small community. As he climbed out of the buggy, Eli figured they'd have one doctor on duty tonight. He just hoped he was inside and not at home waiting for a call.

"I've got Timmy. You should see to your horse, then come inside." Eli spoke quickly to David as he held the little boy in his arms.

David looked panicked. Eli knew the man didn't want to leave his son's side for even a moment. But reason won out over instinct. Since Eli was already turning with Timmy toward the doors and the horse's sides were lathered and heaving from exertion, David nodded his assent.

Without a word, David directed the buggy out of the

way of possible traffic. Eli felt the power of David's trust like a heavy mantle resting across his shoulders. A flash of memory swept over him and he remembered the trust in Shannon's eyes too.

He hurried inside, the wide double doors whooshing open then closing behind him.

"I've got a code blue pediatric case here. We need a rapid response team. Now!" Eli called loud and urgently to the receptionist.

A plump, older woman rushed around the reception counter and reached to look at Timmy's face. She didn't seem to notice Eli's Amish clothing, but a few other people sitting in the waiting room stared with open curiosity. Eli ignored them.

"He's a poison victim. Malathion," Eli spoke to the nurse.

Seeing the urgency of Timmy's condition, the woman waved a hand. "This way."

As Eli followed her, a man wearing a white doctor's coat and a name badge that read *Dr. Graham* ran toward them.

"He's got a shallow pulse, contracted pupils and is breathing with difficulty." Without being asked, Eli rattled off the information, just as he would have done as a paramedic in Denver.

They entered a treatment room and a nurse reached for an oxygen mask. Eli laid Timmy on the bed and opened the quilt so the doctor could get a better look at him.

"What poison are we dealing with here?" Dr. Graham asked in a serious tone, flashing a small handheld light into Timmy's eyes to see how his pupils reacted.

"Malathion," Eli said. "We changed his clothing

since it was spattered with pesticide and bathed him to get the poison off. After that, he started breathing a bit easier."

With a nod, the doctor ordered an antidote while the nurse hooked up an IV. Even being poked by a needle, Timmy didn't move, remaining as still as death. The slow rise and fall of his chest was the only indication that he was still alive.

Eli stepped back, letting the hospital staff take over. Though he was certified, they didn't know him and now wasn't the time to explain. Bracing his back against the wall, he prayed he wasn't too late. As he listened to the doctor giving instructions for the boy's care, Eli had mixed feelings. A part of him missed this action. The thrill of being able to use his expertise to help others. The joy of saving a life. But another part of him was terrified. He might have done something wrong. It had taken so long to get Timmy here.

"Has your son had any convulsions?" Dr. Graham asked, glancing at Eli from over his shoulder.

"He's not my son, but I'm not aware of any convulsions."

The nurse touched Eli's shoulder. "Why don't you wait outside? I'll bring word to you as soon as I can."

He got the message loud and clear. He was in the way.

Stepping out into the reception room, he saw David standing in front of the desk holding his black felt hat in his hands. He looked helpless and confused, glancing around for some sign of his son. When he saw Eli, he showed a relieved expression and hurried over to him. Eli quickly told him what he knew, which wasn't much.

They sat down to wait. Time passed slowly and Eli had too much time to think about his regrets. Leaving Lizzie four years ago was at the top of the list, followed by losing Shannon. But if he hadn't left Lizzie, he never would have met and fallen in love with Shannon. He wouldn't have had his paramedic training or be sitting in this emergency room now.

He wouldn't have known what to do to save Timmy's life.

"I don't know what I'll do if I lose my *sohn*." David leaned forward and covered his face with his hands.

Eli laid a comforting hand on the man's shoulder. He considered the unconditional love of a father and wondered if he would ever have a child of his own. First, he would have to find a wife—and he'd already ruined both of his chances at that. Even though he'd lost both of the women he'd wanted to marry, he could never regret loving them. And that realization surprised him. Loving someone else was deeply personal. Something to be cherished and protected. It was a conscious decision to hold them in your heart for always. And recognizing this gave Eli hope that he might find love a third time. But when he tried to imagine taking a wife, the only one he could picture by his side in the Amish life he'd chosen was Lizzie—and he held very little hope that Lizzie might love him again.

Chapter Eight

Lizzie pulled Ginger into the parking lot of the town park and headed toward a hitching post where a sign read Buggy Parking Only. With the number of Amish families increasing in the area, the town had accommodated them by providing a safe and convenient place with a carport cover for their horses.

Eli had tested Billie and deemed the animal ready for buggy driving again, but Lizzie still felt unsure of the horse. Ginger was older and calmer, so that's the animal she chose for this journey.

Bundled in her heavy winter coat, she hopped out of the buggy. As she tightened the scarf around her neck, she could see puffs of her breath on the chilly air. A skiff of snow that morning hadn't stopped her from coming into Riverton to visit her father and see how Timmy was doing. She'd also stopped off at Ruth Lapp's house for a short visit, happy to find that the woman was over her bronchitis and feeling much better.

Lizzie tied the horse securely, then stepped over to the sidewalk skirting the street. She had just dropped the girls off at school. It hadn't been easy to coax them out of the buggy. They hadn't heard any word on Timmy's condition and were eager to know if the boy was all right. They also were missing their father and wanted to see him. Lizzie couldn't blame them. She also wanted her dad safely at home.

As she walked up the steps to the front of the white brick building, the double doors swished open and she stepped inside. The doors closed and the welcoming warmth enveloped her. She doffed her coat and wiped her damp feet on the large floor mat and looked up.

"Lizzie!"

Linda Albrecht stood in front of the reception counter with her husband, Darrin. He was deep in conversation with the receptionist.

"Have you heard about little Timmy Hostetler?" Linda rushed over to her.

Lizzie nodded eagerly as she removed her gloves. "*Ja*, David brought him to our house last night for Eli's help before coming to the hospital. Is Timmy all right?"

Linda released a deep breath and placed a hand over her heart. "*Ja*, thank the dear Lord. But Eli told us a moment ago that it was a close call."

Darrin Albrecht joined them, folding some papers before tucking them inside the front of his coat.

"Eli is still here?" Lizzie asked.

"He is." The deacon smiled. "He refused to leave Timmy's side until he was sure the boy was okay."

Lizzie wasn't surprised. Eli would undoubtedly want to stay and offer comfort to David if little Timmy had taken a turn for the worse.

"Were you here to visit Timmy?" Lizzie asked.

"*Ne*, we came for a follow-up visit with Dr. McGann," Linda said. "It turns out that Eli was right and Darrin has diabetes. Dr. McGann also prescribed an antibiotic for the wound on Darrin's leg."

Deacon Albrecht nodded. "That's right. Thanks to Eli, the cut is almost completely healed now. Linda has changed our diet, and between that and my diabetes medication, I feel better than I have in months."

Lizzie blinked at this news, remembering that day at church when Eli had advised Deacon Albrecht to go see a doctor soon. Apparently Darrin had accepted Eli's advice and was doing much better because of it.

"I'm so glad the *gut* Lord has blessed you," she said, feeling reluctant to give the credit to Eli. After all, *Gott* provided everything, including Eli's education and knowledge.

"*Ach*, we'd best get moving. We're supposed to have more snow this afternoon and we still have shopping to do. Don't you stay in town too long," Linda admonished.

"*Ne*, I won't," Lizzie promised.

She waved as they hurried outside, both surprised and pleased that Deacon Albrecht was feeling better and Timmy was going to be okay. Thanks to Eli and the schooling *Gott* had provided him with.

She stopped at the reception counter long enough to inquire if Timmy could see visitors, then headed down the hall to his room. She'd stop in briefly before visiting her father.

"It's a good thing you were around or I doubt Timmy would have made it. But I must admit I'm surprised to discover you're a certified paramedic. We don't see many Amish paramedics."

Lizzie turned a corner and came to a dead stop. Standing in the hallway were Eli, David and Dr. Mc-Gann. The doctor lifted a hand and rested it on Eli's shoulder.

"I heard from Dr. Graham that you saved Timmy's life," Dr. McGann continued.

Eli flushed beet red and cast a sheepish glance at the doctor. "The Lord blessed him. I just did what anyone would have done."

"No," David said, speaking in perfect English. "I didn't know what to do. If you hadn't been there, my son might have…"

David didn't finish the statement. His normally stoic expression showed both gratitude and bewilderment as he considered what might have happened to Timmy.

"Thanks to you, a number of the Amish have been coming in to receive medical help. You're a good paramedic and a credit to your people," Dr. McGann said.

"Yes, the Lord has truly blessed us all." Eli turned aside, looking uncomfortable with the praise. His gaze landed on Lizzie and he showed a big smile.

"Lizzie!" he called, looking relieved by the distraction.

She hurried forward, not knowing what to make of all that she'd overheard. Also, being near Eli caused a buzz of excitement to course through her body.

"I'm sorry I wasn't there to milk the cows this morning, but I didn't have a ride home," Eli said.

She shook her head. "Don't worry about it. You had more important things to do here. I understand that Timmy is going to be all right."

She couldn't prevent a note of cheerfulness from

filling her voice. All that mattered right now was that the boy was going to live.

"Ja." David nodded happily. "He'll have to stay here a couple of more days, just to make sure he's breathing okay on his own, but he reacted well to the antidote."

"Dr. McGann, this is Lizzie Beiler, a member of our congregation." Eli made the introductions.

"Yes, Ms. Beiler and I know each other already. I've been treating her father." The doctor showed a kind smile.

"That's right. How is he doing?" she asked.

"Very good. The swelling has gone down and I think we'll be able to cast his leg tomorrow morning. He can go home the day after that. But he'll need several more weeks of bed rest before resuming his usual activities. If you want to drive in on Thursday morning, he should be ready to go home then."

"Oh, that's *wundervoll!*" Lizzie exclaimed.

Two more days and her father would be home. What a relief!

"And now, I'd better get back to work." With a gesture of farewell, Dr. McGann headed down the hall.

"And I'm going to go back in with Timmy. Thanks again, my dear friend. And thanks to Lizzie as well." David reached out and shook Eli's hand as he winked at Lizzie, then he turned and entered a room.

Lizzie peered inside and saw Timmy lying on the hospital bed, his eyes closed in sleep. Covered by a thin blanket, he wore an oxygen mask, but she could see the easy rising and falling of his tiny chest.

"And I had better go see my *vadder.*" Lizzie stepped around Eli, but paused when he briefly touched her arm.

"Would you mind giving me a ride back to your

farm when you're finished? I used David's cell phone last night to call my *vadder* and tell him where I am, but I came into town with David and my horse and buggy are still at your place," he said.

"Of course. I won't be long. I heard that a snow-storm is headed our way and I need to pick the girls up from school before we go home."

He nodded and she hurried on her way, still feeling the warmth of his fingers on her arm.

Jeremiah was sitting up eating lunch when she stepped into his room. He set a carton of milk on his tray and reached out a hand to her.

"Lizzie! Did you bring me any homemade bread? I'm half-starved for your cooking," he said.

She laughed. "I'm afraid not, but it looks like you'll be home in a couple of days, so you can eat all the bread you want soon." She leaned over and hugged him tight, his words pleasing her enormously. A quick glance at his filled plate told her why he wasn't happy with the hospital food. She had to admit, she wouldn't be interested, either.

"How are the *maed*?" he asked after her sisters.

"*Gut*. They wanted to come with, to see you and how Timmy is doing, but I insisted they go to school." She quickly told him about the close call last night and all that Dr. McGann had said about Eli saving the child's life.

"*Ja*, Deacon Albrecht visited me earlier and told me Timmy will be all right."

"The doctor credits Eli with helping Deacon Albrecht get on top of his diabetes too," she said.

"Hmm." Jeremiah looked skeptical.

"The Lord moves in mysterious ways. Perhaps He

used Eli to do His *gut* work here on earth," she suggested.

And if that was the case, wasn't it also possible that the Lord had provided the opportunity for Eli to gain higher learning, so that he could serve others in such a manner? Lizzie didn't pose the question to her father. She knew better than to push the issue, even if Eli's education had saved Timmy's life and helped other members of their *Gmay*.

"*Ja*, it is possible." Jeremiah's voice sounded rather gruff and disapproving.

Sitting in a chair next to her father's bed, she chatted with him about the farm. Finally, Lizzie asked a question that had been weighing heavily on her mind of late.

"When he first went to Denver, Eli said he left me a letter of goodbye. He also said he sent many other letters to me, yet I've never received any. Do you know something about this?" she asked.

Jeremiah's eyes widened and he took a deep breath, taking time to choose his words carefully. A sick feeling settled inside Lizzie's stomach and she dreaded his answer.

"*Ja*, I know about the letters." Lifting his head, Jeremiah met her gaze, his forehead set in a stubborn frown. "I feared Eli might entice you to join him in the *Englisch* world, so I sent all the letters back to him unopened."

So. Eli had told her the truth. He'd tried to say goodbye to her after all. A part of her was relieved that he hadn't lied. That he hadn't abandoned her without a single word. And yet, another part of her was angry that she'd been denied the truth for all this time. Eli had his reasons for leaving, but her father's deception hurt her deeply. A feeling of righteous indignation clogged her throat and she gripped her hands together in her lap, trying not to be angry.

"You had no right to hide my letters," she said.

"I know. Please don't think harshly of me, *dochder*. As your *vadder*, I did what I thought was best, because I love you and didn't want to lose you."

Her heart softened. She couldn't really fault her father's actions. By hiding Eli's letters, he'd only been trying to protect her. To keep her in their faith, with their family.

"You should have trusted me more. I'm a grown woman and the choice to stay or go be with Eli was mine alone to make," she said.

He looked away, licking his dried lips. "I couldn't take that chance. Knowing how much you loved Eli, I feared you might go."

She shook her head. "You might have been surprised. I love my *familye* and my faith dearly too."

He looked at her, his gruff face lined with fatigue. "If I had given you Eli's letters, would you have left?"

She shrugged. "It doesn't matter now. It's in the past."

Yet, she didn't really know the answer. Four years was a long time and yet it was no time at all. She had only been seventeen. She had felt so grown up, and yet since that time, she had changed so much. Her heart had been broken, but her faith had grown. Her *familye* had come to mean more than anything to her, and she knew now that their community was where she belonged. Yet, she wasn't sure if she would have stayed back then. And knowing about the letters changed nothing between her and Eli. He had left. They'd grown apart. Now, their priorities were different. But she had to be honest with herself. She might have gone with Eli. Her love for him had been so strong that she might have put aside her faith and become *Englisch* in order to be with him. But it didn't matter now because she would never know.

The buggy bounced through a mud puddle in the rutted road leading to the schoolhouse. Eli gripped the lead lines tighter and breathed a thankful sigh that they were nearly there. With everything that had happened last night, he hadn't slept at all. He'd been too worried about Timmy. Fatigue hadn't set it until this morning, when he was assured the boy would recover. Now, Eli felt a mixture of lethargy and relief. A few more hours and he'd be able to rest. But first, he had to make sure Lizzie and the girls arrived home safe and all was well on their farm.

"There's Marty." Lizzie pointed as they rode into the school yard.

Eli pulled the buggy to a stop in front of the one-room red log building. Constructed by the men of their *Gmay*, the schoolhouse had come from a kit they'd ordered a number of years earlier. Surrounded by a chain-link fence, the property included a small baseball field and sat in the farthest corner of Bishop Yoder's hayfield.

"Lizzie!" The girl waved.

Taking Annie's hand, both children ran toward them. Several other kids followed along with Rebecca Geingerich, their teacher. No doubt they'd all heard from Marty and Annie about Timmy's accident and were eager to know if he was all right.

"Have you just come from town? Any news of Timmy?" Rebecca asked in an anxious tone, holding her shawl tightly around her shoulders.

Eli nodded. "*Ja*, and he is going to be just fine."

The children listened eagerly as Eli and Lizzie related all that had happened. A few parents who were picking up their kids also paused, seeking the news.

"It was *gut* you were there when David needed you," one man exclaimed.

"*Ja*, little Timmy might not have made it without you," Rebecca said.

Eli waved a hand, feeling embarrassed by the praise. "The *gut* Lord saw us through. It was *Gott*'s will that Timmy survive."

"*Ja*, it was *Gott*'s will." They all nodded in agreement.

As Eli helped Marty and Annie into the buggy, he knew word would soon spread across the entire *Gmay* about what had happened. Eli really believed what he said. Truly, the Lord had blessed them. This time.

He could take no credit for the child's recovery. In fact, he'd believed Timmy would die. At the very least, the boy should have suffered permanent damage to his lungs. Yet he was thriving and even breathing on his own. Eli never should have doubted the Lord's power. But why hadn't *Gott* saved Shannon? Why did she have to die?

Pondering the inequality, Eli slapped the leads against Ginger's back. He glanced at the gray sky overhead, which mirrored his doubtful feelings.

Marty smiled brightly. "I'm so happy Timmy is gonna be okay."

"Me too," Annie spoke with a contented sigh.

As the buggy sped along the county road, it started to snow. Big, heavy flakes laden with moisture. Reaching out a hand to wipe off the front storm window so he could see out, Eli was eager to get Lizzie and her sisters home safely. He was grateful the buggy had thin glass to protect them from the elements, but he sure missed the windshield wipers of a car.

In the back seat, the two little girls exclaimed about the snow. Cocooned by the sheltering walls of the buggy, they nestled beneath a warm blanket. Soon, their eyelids drooped and they dozed off.

Casting a quick glance over her shoulder, Lizzie smiled with satisfaction. "They didn't sleep well last night. I'm afraid everyone in the *Gmay* has been worried about Timmy."

"*Ja*, his condition was pretty serious," Eli agreed.

"My *vadder* should be able to come home on Thursday," she said, then related what the doctor had told her.

"*Gut*. The storm will have passed by then, but the roads may still be slick. I'd feel better if you let me drive you into town to pick him up from the hospital."

She nodded. "I would appreciate that. I'm not sure I can lift him in and out of the buggy by myself. He won't be able to walk for several weeks."

"It's no problem. I'll help you."

She nodded and a long, swelling silence followed.

"You seem deep in thought today. Is everything all right at the farm?" he finally asked.

"*Ja*, all is well." Her voice sounded small and she tugged her black traveling bonnet closer around her face.

They rode in quiet for several more minutes before Eli couldn't take it any longer.

"Is something troubling you?" he asked.

Finally, she glanced his way. "I… I spoke to my *vadder* about your letters."

A leaden weight settled in Eli's chest. "And?"

"And he confessed that he sent them all back to you." She hurried on. "I hope you won't think unkindly of him. He's very sorry for not telling me about them, but he feared I might leave and join you in Denver. He only wanted what was best for me."

Hmm. Just as Eli had suspected.

"But what about what you wanted?" he asked with a brief glance in her direction. In this weather, he was unwilling to take his eyes off the road for long.

She took a deep inhale and let it go. "I guess we'll never know now."

True. It was water under the bridge. But Lizzie's voice sounded embarrassed, as if she hated confessing her father's duplicity. Because of the situation, Eli couldn't bring himself to be angry over Jeremiah's misdeed. Not when he had so many faults of his own to repent from.

"It's all right," he said. "I probably would have done the same thing if you had been my *dochder*. I can't blame Jeremiah for wanting what he believes is best for you."

She looked at him. "*Danke*. I appreciate your understanding."

"When I didn't hear from you, I figured you didn't love me anymore," he said. "I felt terrible about that, but then I realized I had to move on with my life. I… I met an *Englisch* girl and…and I asked her to marry me."

The words slipped out before he could stop them. Lizzie jerked around, her eyes round with shock. He wondered if he'd made a huge mistake by telling her, but also felt relieved to finally tell someone about Shannon. Because he feared their censure, he hadn't even told his parents about her.

"You…you were engaged to be married? To an *Englisch* woman?" she asked, her voice sounding small and deflated.

He nodded and suddenly the story poured out of him. He told Lizzie everything. How he'd given up on ever hearing from her again. How he'd met Shannon when she was working at the hospital as a pediatric volunteer. How gentle, kind and reserved she was and how they'd dated some time before becoming engaged. And then about the drunk driving accident after which she'd died in his arms.

He stared straight ahead and gripped the lead lines tighter as he spoke in a low, hoarse voice. "She was driving the car that night when a drunk driver hit us head-on. She survived the initial impact and I thought she'd be all right, but I… I couldn't save her, Lizzie. She was bleeding internally and I couldn't stop it. I prayed so hard, but *Gott* didn't answer me. He let Shannon die."

Lizzie must have heard the anguish in his voice, because she pressed her gloved fingers against her lips. He was surprised to see tears shimmering in her eyes.

"*Ach*, Eli. I'm so sorry for your loss, but I have no doubt the Lord was with you that night. We don't always understand His ways, but He has our best interests in mind. There was nothing else you could have done. It wasn't your fault. You know that, don't you?" Her voice was filled with sincerity, her eyes crinkled with compassion.

No, he didn't know that. He kept replaying everything in his mind, as if in slow motion. Trying to think of what steps he might have taken to help Shannon survive.

They were quiet for several moments, listening to the gusts of wind as white swirled around them. The falling snow was getting worse. Ginger lowered her head and trudged onward, her horseshoes biting into the slick sheet of ice covering the road. Without the protection of doors and windows, they would all be truly miserable right now.

"You must have loved Shannon very much," Lizzie said.

He nodded. "I did, just as I loved you."

She stiffened beside him and he feared she might be angry. But when he glanced over, he saw nothing but sympathy in her eyes.

"It wasn't your fault, Eli. Accidents happen and you can't save everyone. We have to trust in *Gott*. He knows what is best for each of us. You must believe that."

Somehow the conviction in her voice made him feel better. Yet, knowing how he'd broken her heart, he was surprised she was offering him comfort. If anything, he deserved her anger. But that wasn't her way.

"When you left, I was hurt to think that you could forget me so easily," she continued. "But now, I understand what happened. You wanted to know more about the world, to learn and grow. It was your choice to go and I mustn't judge you for that. It wasn't your fault that *Daed* hid your letters from me. And I can't hold a grudge against Shannon and the love you shared with her either."

"I… I tried so hard to save her," he said, trying not

to let his emotions show in his wobbly voice. But he couldn't seem to help it. He had to quickly wipe his eyes.

"Of course you did." She rested a gloved hand on his arm, her touch consoling. "I know you did everything you could. But now, you should hand your pain over to the Lord. Give your grief to Him and be at peace."

She withdrew her hand and became very still, her brow furrowed in a troubled frown. She seemed so understanding. So supportive. It reminded him of when they were teenagers and she'd always put everyone else first. Her generous spirit had been one of the things he'd loved the most about her.

A particularly hard gust rocked the buggy and drew his attention back to the road ahead. He had to reach outside and clear the caking snow off the window. The wind buffeted them. For just a moment, he missed the comfort of an automobile's heater and defroster, not to mention the solid security of the larger, heavier vehicles. But a car wouldn't include Lizzie. Dear, faithful Lizzie.

He felt strangely calm sitting next to her. As he drew his arm back inside, he caught her worried look.

"I'll sure be glad when we're home," she said. "I thought we could beat the storm. I have to admit I'm glad you're driving instead of me."

In spite of her smile, her body seemed stiff and her demeanor reserved. Perhaps he was reading something in her manner that wasn't really there. As she shivered and pulled a blanket over her legs, he figured she was just worried about the weather. Yes, that must be it.

"You're *willkomm*," he replied, feeling better, yet feeling worse at the same time. Oh, he was so confused. He didn't know himself anymore. Didn't know where he belonged or what he wanted.

Fearing a truck might come barreling down the road and not see them in the storm, he pulled the horse as far over onto the shoulder as he dared. Through the white swirling around them, he could just make out the jutting edges of an irrigation ditch running parallel to the road. He eyed the reflective snowplow poles and mileage markers, using them as a guide to stay out of the ditch. As he concentrated on his driving, they didn't speak for several minutes. A comfortable silence settled over them, something he hadn't realized how much he'd missed…until now. But he had little time to consider the reason why as they came upon a car that had slid off the road.

Chapter Nine

Two thin lines on the icy road showed where the tires of the black car had skidded off the road. The vehicle's hazard lights blinked red. Through the flurries of wind gusting against the falling snow, Lizzie could make out the front fender hanging just above the irrigation ditch. Another inch and the vehicle would drop two feet and require a tow truck to drag it out.

Lizzie clutched the side of the buggy, a feeling of trepidation filling her heart. The last time she'd been involved in a car accident had not been pleasant. Even as she wished they didn't have to stop, she knew they must. They couldn't pass by someone in need.

Eli pulled Ginger to a halt just behind the floundered car. "Wait here inside the buggy. I'll see if we can help."

Pulling his black felt hat lower over his forehead, Eli opened the door and stepped out into the lashing wind and snow. Chilling air whooshed inside the buggy. As she looked out at several tall elm trees edging the road, their barren limbs covered in white, she thought the winter scene would be beautiful…if she were watching it from the safety of her kitchen window. But sitting inside a horse-drawn buggy, she couldn't help wishing they were anywhere but here.

Hunching his wide shoulders, Eli hurried toward the car. Lizzie's gaze followed him. For some odd reason, she felt desperate to keep her eyes on him. As if she'd lose him again if she couldn't see him anymore.

At the car, Eli leaned forward and someone inside the vehicle rolled down a window to speak with him. Although Lizzie couldn't hear their conversation, she saw Eli gesture toward the horse and nod several times.

"What's going on?" Awakened by the stop, Annie rubbed her eyes and sat up.

Marty leaned forward, her eyes wide with fear. "We didn't wreck again, did we?"

Lizzie swiveled in her seat and smiled. *"Ne, bensel,"* she reassured them. "There's just a car off the road and Eli is seeing if they need our help."

A strong surge of wind rocked the buggy. Staring out the thin windows, Annie shivered and her eyes welled with tears. "But I wanna go home. I don't wanna be out here anymore."

"Me either. Let's go home now," Marty cried.

Lizzie reached back and consoled both girls, pulling them close for a quick kiss on their cheeks. *"Ne, my liebchen,* we must help these people if we can. But don't worry. *Gott* will take care of us. And Eli won't let any harm befall us."

As she cuddled her sisters, she froze at what she'd said. Did she really trust Eli so much? Since he'd arrived home, he'd shown sound judgment, but she still doubted him. He'd told her about his *Englisch* girlfriend and her heart ached for all that he'd lost. But it hurt Lizzie deeply to know he'd loved someone else so much. That he'd made a life without her. Now he was back. But did she trust him to stay? She wasn't sure.

When he jerked open the door and leaned inside, she whirled around. His hat, shoulders and arms were covered with snow. Icy drops of water covered his face. He wiped them away with a brush of his hand, his breath puffing on the frigid air. Lizzie hated that he had to be out in this rotten weather.

"I'm going to see if Ginger can pull the car back onto the road. I want all of you to stay inside, out of the wet and cold," he said.

Lizzie nodded, grateful for his consideration. But something in her expression must have betrayed her thoughts.

"Don't worry. It's going to be all right. We're just making memories to laugh about later." He flashed her a confident smile, then shut the door.

Annie shivered at the blast of frigid air. "Brr! I'm glad Eli is taking care of this. I'd hate to be outside right now."

"Me too," Marty said.

Me three! Lizzie thought. Her respect for Eli grew when she saw that he didn't complain or shirk his responsibilities. He was a man who didn't flinch at what had to be done.

They watched as he unhitched Ginger from the buggy. An *Englisch* man in a pair of blue jeans and a light jacket got out of the car to help. Without a hat or gloves to protect him from the elements, the *Englischer* hunched his shoulders and mostly just shielded his face from the snow while Eli did the work. Lizzie figured he had no idea how to harness a horse let alone tie the lines to the car. In contrast, Eli moved with speed and confidence. She wondered how he could see what he was doing in the lashing storm. But soon, he had the horse hooked up and she couldn't help thinking that he'd become an amazing man.

He spoke to the *Englischer*, seeming completely comfortable around the stranger. While Lizzie preferred not to mingle with the *Englisch*, she supposed Eli was used to them and their strange ways. A part of her disapproved of his life among them, but right now, she appreciated his goodness and generosity.

Within moments, the *Englischer* climbed back into his vehicle and put it in Reverse. Through the rear window, Lizzie saw two young children peering out, their faces pale, their eyes round. A woman's face was visible, looking back from the front seat, and Lizzie realized an entire *Englisch familye* was inside the car.

With Eli directing the horse, Ginger leaned forward, her hooves digging into the snow as she pulled on the line. The animal's back was blanketed with white, but she seemed not to notice.

The vehicle's tires made a whizzing sound as they spun around. Finally, they caught traction and the car moved back a space. Eli led Ginger out of the way as the car came to a rest on the icy pavement.

"You see?" Marty nudged Annie. "Eli isn't worried one bit, so we shouldn't be either."

Annie nodded, huddling closer to her sister. "*Ja*, the *gut* Lord would want us to stop and help our neighbors, even if they are *Englisch* and we're afraid."

Tears filled Lizzie's eyes and she quickly wiped them away so the girls wouldn't see. Her siblings sounded so confident and grown-up that it touched her heart. She could learn from their generous and trusting example. Their words inspired her to have courage and believe in Eli too. After all, he'd stopped to help in spite of the hardship and discomfort to himself. He'd already done so much for her *familye* and many other people in their *Gmay* too. From all appearances, Eli was a good, devout Amish man. He'd suffered a lot recently. When he'd told her about losing his fiancée, he'd seemed so lost and hurt. Lizzie didn't have the heart to be angry with him anymore. She had to accept that he didn't love her. That he'd moved on and found another life that didn't include her. She should move on too. But would he stay? Or would he recover from his loss and decide the Amish life wasn't for him after all? Already, Lizzie cared too much about him. She told herself it was normal to care for everyone in the *Gmay*. But if Lizzie wasn't careful, she could get her heart broken again.

Eli climbed back into the buggy and breathed a sigh of relief. Conscious of Lizzie watching him, he blew onto his gloved hands, trying to warm them. Without being asked, Lizzie handed him a blanket. He wiped his damp face.

"Wrap it over your body. It'll warm you up quicker," she said.

"Danke," he murmured, startled to hear a croak in his voice. He coughed, hoping he didn't get hypothermia for his good deeds.

When he had the blanket packed tight around his upper torso and thighs, he felt better and shivered less. He cleared his voice and took hold of the lead lines. "Mark Walden and his *familye* are in the car.

Mrs. Walden is five months pregnant and they're very grateful that we stopped."

Lizzie nodded. "*Ja*, it was the right thing to do."

He swallowed, grateful to be out of the wet and cold. "The Waldens are going to accompany us to the farm, just to ensure we arrive safely. Would you rather ride in their warm car while I drive the buggy?"

Lizzie shook her head. "That's very kind of them, but I'd rather stay with you." She glanced back at the girls, still huddled together beneath a heavy quilt. "I believe we are warm enough."

Eli wasn't surprised by her decision. He'd been living among the *Englisch* and was comfortable around them. But Lizzie wasn't.

"All right. They'll drive ahead of us, so that their lights can show the way."

He wasn't sure, but he thought he saw a flicker of relief fill her eyes before she looked away. Releasing the brake, he called loudly to Ginger, fearing the horse couldn't hear him above the storm. Either she caught his command or the animal felt the leads against her back, because she leaned into the harness, dug in her hooves and pulled forward. Eli felt the grating of the buggy wheels, frozen in ice. They gave way and were soon moving at a smooth pace. The black car drove in front of them, going slow. The bright taillights of the vehicle helped Eli see the way in the falling snow.

"I'll be glad when we're home," Marty sniffled.

"Me too. I don't want to do any more good deeds today," Annie said, her voice trembling.

"*Ja*, do you think we'll make it okay?" Lizzie asked.

Focusing on the road, Eli didn't look at any of them, but he felt the girls crouched forward between him and Lizzie. A little hand rested on his shoulder and he thought it must be Annie's. He imagined each child's eyes were wide with fear and a protective feeling filled his chest with warmth and compassion. He'd do almost anything to keep these three girls safe and wanted to reassure them all.

"Of course we'll make it," he said. "We're going very slow. Don't worry. With the Waldens' car to light the way, we'll be there soon enough." But a little doubt nibbled at his mind. Even at this snail's pace, he could see the Waldens' vehicle skidding on the icy road. Now and then, he could feel the buggy doing the same and he didn't want any mishaps to make matters worse. At this pace, the worst that could happen was they'd end up on the side of the road…unless a truck or car came up too fast behind them. That could end in catastrophe and he wondered if he should have insisted the girls ride in the safety of the car.

Everyone in the buggy was incredibly quiet. They each seemed to know that he needed to concentrate on his driving. In his heart, Eli whispered a prayer for their safety.

As they rode in silence, his thoughts began to wander. He wished he had the courage to confide another serious issue to Lizzie.

The day before, he'd received another letter from Tom Caldwell, his former employer in Denver. Tom had sent a new job offer for Eli to become an EMT supervisor. Before he lost Shannon, Eli would have loved to make such a career move. When he'd first read the letter, his heart had leaped at the proposal. It would be a wonderful way to use his skills to serve others. But then, he remembered the commitment he'd made to *Gott* and his *familye*. He planned to be baptized soon. He loved the Lord and wanted to stay in Riverton. Didn't he?

If only there was a way for him to work as a paramedic and remain here among his people. But he didn't see how. To be a paramedic, he'd need to keep his certifications current, which meant taking yearly classes and using modern technology. Surely the elders of his church would never approve of that, especially Jeremiah, who was the minister of their congregation. Eli didn't even dare ask. Not when he'd been home such a short time. They might think he wasn't serious about staying. And he was. Yet, he felt torn.

By the time they pulled into the yard of the Beilers' farm, it was early evening and the snow had stopped. They'd passed two big plows up on the county road and knew the pavement would be cleared by morning.

Eli released a giant whoosh, his breath looking like a puff of smoke on the air. He hadn't realized he'd been holding his breath. They were safe. He'd kept his promise to Lizzie and the girls.

"We're home!" Marty crowed with delight.

"*Ja*, we're safe," Lizzie said, her voice a soft whisper.

Mark Walden waved as he slowly turned his car around and headed back toward the county road so he could take his *familye* home.

"But what if they go off the road again?" Annie asked, watching their red taillights fade into the darkness.

"They won't. *Gott* is with all of us tonight and they're driving nice and slow. They also have a cell phone to call for help. They'll arrive just fine," Eli said, hoping his words were true.

"*Ja*, we must trust in *Gott* to keep us safe, even when we don't have a cell phone," Lizzie said.

Eli wasn't certain, but he thought he saw her lips curve into a little smile. Her sense of humor made him chuckle.

He pulled up in front of the dark house. "You take the *maed* inside and I'll take Ginger to the barn. I want to feed and dry her off *gut*. Then I'll head on home."

Lizzie's mouth dropped open. "But it's not safe for you to travel tonight. You should stay here until morning."

"It wouldn't be appropriate. I'll be fine. The snow has stopped. Once I get up to the county road, the plows will have cleared the asphalt all the way to my *eldres'* farm. And it would be unseemly for me to stay here tonight when you and the *maed* are alone."

She looked away, her gaze suddenly shy. "*Ach*, I hadn't thought about that. But you are right."

Eli nodded, wishing he dared take just a moment to seek her advice. Her compassion over Shannon's death had touched him deeply. Lizzie had always been so empathetic and kind. So obedient and wise. But he had no illusions. Lizzie would never approve of him asking their leaders to sanction his work as a paramedic. Especially if she knew he was considering accepting another job offer in Denver. Leaving Riverton meant abandoning his faith and *familye* again, something he hated to do. Because the next time he left, he knew he would never be coming back.

Chapter Ten

A freezing rain the next day, followed by another day of warm sunshine, cleared the snow and ice off the roads. A blanket of white still covered the valley and mountains surrounding them and another storm was on its way. Since they needed the water so badly for their summer irrigation, Lizzie wouldn't complain. Especially since they had good weather right now, when she needed it most. Standing in her father's hospital room in town, she glanced out the window and noticed the morning sky was still clear. They had just enough time to get him home. The chill air made her pull her heavy cape tighter around her.

"I don't know why you let Eli drive you into town. Couldn't you have come to get me on your own?" Jeremiah grumbled. He sat on the edge of the bed, fully dressed, his casted leg extended in front of him.

"*Ne, Daedi*. The weather has been too bad and I'm not sure I can lift you alone." She'd already told him about getting caught in a blizzard the night they'd helped pull the *familye*'s car back onto the road.

"What about Martin Hostetler? Couldn't he drive you into town instead of Eli?"

Lizzie clenched her eyes shut at the thought. Tall and slender, with bright red hair and a smattering of freckles, Martin was a nice enough man, but a bit too zealous for her. His outgoing nature and forward manner always unnerved Lizzie. He was too overt and outspoken for her likes. After Eli had left, it had taken a year to convince Martin that she wasn't interested in courting with him. The last thing she wanted to do was encourage him by asking if he would drive her into town to pick up her father.

"Bishop Yoder specifically charged Eli with looking after the farm and our *familye*. I'm afraid we have no choice but to accept his help," she said.

There. That was good. Surely her father wouldn't argue with the bishop.

"Has Eli...has he been spending quite a bit of time with you while I've been in the hospital?" Jeremiah asked.

"*Ne*, he mostly works outside or in the barn."

Not to mention her numerous efforts to avoid him.

After the doctor had instructed them on some exercises Jeremiah could do at home to help quicken his rehabilitation, she'd packed her father's few belongings into a bag. Eli had taken it outside as he went to fetch the horse and buggy. Her two sisters had tagged along with Eli, holding his hands and smiling. Now, Lizzie and her father were just waiting for an orderly to bring a wheelchair so they could wheel her father outside.

"So, he hasn't spoken to you about going back to the *Englisch* world with him?" Jeremiah peered at her with a look that said he didn't want to intrude, but he couldn't help asking anyway.

She snorted. "Don't worry, *Vadder*. Eli and I have no interest in each other anymore. He's been a tremendous help and looked after the farm, but he's been nothing but completely appropriate the entire time."

She didn't dare tell him about Shannon, Eli's fiancée—the proof that he'd fully moved past his old feelings for her. Though Eli hadn't asked her to keep the information private, she got the impression he had confided in her and she didn't want to betray that trust.

"*Ach*, what's taking so long?" Jeremiah looked at the door, a surly frown on his face.

Since her father was normally a gentle, patient man, Lizzie surmised that his weariness with the hospital was the reason for his impatience.

"They'll be here soon," she soothed.

Her own composure surprised her. But something had changed inside of her since Eli had told her about Shannon. When she'd reassured him that his fiancée's death wasn't his fault, a startling realization had struck her. She must exercise what she preached and hand her own grief and anger over to the Lord. It was what *Gott* expected from her. Eli had suffered enough without her condemnation too. But her heart still ached with the knowledge that he'd gotten over his love for her, and had been ready to build a life with Shannon. And that hurt most of all.

Thankfully, a young man wearing a blue smock wheeled a chair into the room at that moment.

"All ready to go?" the orderly asked in a pleasant voice. Lizzie could see from his curious gaze that he found their Amish clothing interesting, but he didn't say anything.

"We've been ready for half an hour," Jeremiah grumbled.

The orderly stepped forward, seeming unruffled by Jeremiah's bad humor. "Then let's get you on your way home. Remember not to put any weight on your casted leg."

Jeremiah nodded, reaching out as the orderly wrapped his arms around him to take the brunt of his weight before hefting him into the seat. An extender bar was lifted into place and Jeremiah's casted leg rested outstretched on the support.

"All ready?" The orderly smiled at Lizzie.

She nodded and he pushed the chair out of the room and down the long hall. Tugging her black bonnet lower over her forehead, Lizzie followed behind. As they passed Timmy's room, she glanced inside, finding the bed vacant. Jeremiah had told her the boy had gone home just before she'd arrived. Knowing the child was healthy enough to return to his *familye* brought a buoyant feeling to Lizzie's chest.

Outside, the frigid air caught her breath and she took a quick inhale. The horse and buggy were waiting at the bottom of the steps. The orderly wheeled Jeremiah down a side ramp sprinkled with ice melt. Eli hopped out of the buggy and came to assist.

"This young man can get me in just fine." Jeremiah gave Eli the cold shoulder by turning toward the orderly.

"Of course," Eli said, gracious as always but looking a bit snubbed by the rebuttal.

While Eli stood on the sidewalk, Lizzie stared at her

father in amazement. She knew her father was suspicious of the other man, but what cause did he have to be so rude to Eli? It wasn't like her father. No, not at all. She sensed that something was bothering him and she had no idea what it was.

The orderly lifted Jeremiah into the buggy, then gripped the handles on the wheelchair and nodded farewell.

"Drive safely," he called.

Eli waved before reaching to help Lizzie into the back of the buggy with her two sisters. She looked inside and found that little Annie had twined her hand around her father's arm and beamed with pleasure to know he was finally going home.

As always, Eli took hold of Lizzie's arm so she wouldn't stumble on the wet footrest. Normally, she looked away and tried to ignore how his touch made her stomach quiver. But this time, their gazes met. In his eyes, she saw a flash of uncertainty, then it was gone and she thought she must have imagined it. After all, Eli was the strongest, most confident man she knew. Surely her father's temper hadn't rattled him.

Once Eli was inside, he took up the lead lines and slapped them against Billie's back. The buggy jerked forward as the horse took off at a slow trot out of the parking lot. While the little girls jabbered about their activities to their father, the adults were quiet. From the stiff shoulders of the two men sitting in front, Lizzie could feel the tension in the air like a thick fog. She understood *Daed*'s motives for keeping Eli's letters from her, but she didn't understand why he was offish toward Eli now. Unless *Daed* was like Marva Geingerich and feared Eli might leave again…and try to take

Lizzie with him. He'd already asked Lizzie about it, so that must be the problem. But it wasn't becoming of *Daed* to be so judgmental.

The ride home seemed to take much longer than usual. By the time they arrived, all the adults seemed to be in a sour mood. The children, picking up on the tension but not understanding it, seemed anxious and confused, bewildered as to why the happy occasion of their father coming home wasn't being treated with more joy.

Without a word, Lizzie hurried up the front steps to hold the house's door open for Eli. Since she wasn't strong enough, *Daed* had no option but to let the other man help him inside. The night before, Eli had been kind enough to move *Daed*'s bed downstairs to the living room. Lizzie figured her father wouldn't be able to negotiate the stairs. Having him close at hand would make it easier to see to his needs too.

"I can remove your shoe so you can lie down," Annie offered as Eli deposited her father on the narrow bed.

Jeremiah sat straight as a board. "I don't want my shoe removed. I should be outside working."

Showing her sternest frown, Lizzie placed her hands on her hips and shook her head. "There will be no working or putting weight on your injured leg for several more weeks. The doctor said if you don't want to walk with a limp, you'll let the bones heal."

"*Ja*, and I'll take care of the farm work," Eli said.

Jeremiah glanced at the younger man. "What work have you already done?"

Eli stood in front of Jeremiah, holding his hat in his hands. While Lizzie helped her sisters doff their coats and gloves, Eli recounted a few of the things he'd done, including mending the fence, shoeing the horses and a myriad of other chores.

"And don't forget baling and putting away the hay," Lizzie said as she hung their coats in the closet. She headed toward the kitchen, wanting to be alone for some reason. With her sisters here to mind their father, she decided to start lunch.

"Humph," came her father's surly reply. "I'm glad you've been of use then. I guess you didn't forget how to bale a field during all that time you were living among the *Englisch*."

Again, Lizzie was surprised by the extent of her father's poor manners.

"*Ne*, sir. I remember very well how to plow and bale and I'm glad I could help you out," Eli replied.

Lizzie caught the teasing quality in Eli's voice. She'd never seen a man work as hard as he had worked for them. No doubt he was feeling amused by Jeremiah's skepticism. And that made her want to defend him to her father and she didn't understand why. Yes, she was grateful to Eli. His presence on the farm had brought her a lot of comfort. Because of him, her burdens had been eased but… Oh, she didn't know what to think anymore. Eli didn't love her anymore and all her crazy feelings would lead to nothing.

Whew! After getting the third degree from Jeremiah, Eli was glad to escape the house. Lizzie would call him for the noon meal soon, but he thought going hungry might be better than facing her father again. The man obviously didn't like him and Eli understood why. As teenagers, he and Lizzie had been inseparable. Everyone expected them to marry. But then, he'd left and Jeremiah had hidden his letters from Lizzie. No doubt the man feared, then and now, that Eli might contaminate her with his *Englisch* ideas.

Opening the barn door, Eli stepped inside, relieved to be alone. He wanted to feel angry at Jeremiah, but he couldn't. Losing Shannon had taught him a patience he didn't quite understand. He only knew that everyone was a child of *Gott*. Everyone made mistakes. But he deeply believed in the power of the Atonement and forgiveness. Otherwise, he wouldn't have come home. And frankly, he was tired of being angry.

"Eli?"

He whirled around and found Lizzie standing just inside the doorway. Sunlight glimmered behind her, highlighting several strands of golden hair that had escaped her prayer bonnet. Her forehead was furrowed with concern. Wearing her winter cape, her porcelain cheeks had a rosy hue, as if they'd been kissed by the cold air. And for just a moment, he thought about taking her into his arms and kissing her. And that thought confused him. He still loved Shannon, didn't he? How could he be thinking about Lizzie when his fiancée had so recently died?

"I brought you something to eat," she said.

For the first time, he noticed that she held a tray covered by a white dish towel.

She came forward and set the tray on a wooden bench. Stepping back, she smoothed her cape, looking suddenly shy.

"I figured you wouldn't want to eat in the house today. My *vadder* isn't in a very *gut* mood," she said.

How insightful of her, but he didn't say so. *"Danke."*

Now! Now he should tell her about the job offer in Denver. He'd been pondering the letter he'd received from Tom Caldwell for days now, but still had found no answers. He was alone with Lizzie and it was a perfect moment to seek her advice.

"Are you all right?" she asked, her expression earnest.

"Sure. I'm fine." He smiled, hoping to alleviate her fears. It occurred to him that he hadn't seen her smile all day. She must have a lot on her mind too and he wished he could do even more to alleviate her load. He remembered how close they'd been as teenagers and a part of him wished they could share that closeness again.

She poked a clump of hay with the tip of her shoe. "I… I'm sure *Daed* will feel better tomorrow."

He lifted his head. "He's upset because I'm here. I've been living among the *Englisch* and he thinks I might corrupt you."

Her mouth dropped open. "He doesn't think that at all."

"Doesn't he?" he challenged.

She ducked her head, a mingling of acceptance and dismay in her eyes. "*Ach*, maybe a little bit. I'll speak to him."

"*Ne*, let it go. I knew when I returned that I'd have to prove myself again."

She met his eyes. "Can you blame him for not trusting you? You ran away. You've been gone a long time."

"*Ja*, you're right. I can't blame anyone for being upset with me. In fact, you might be even more disappointed when you hear that I've received a job offer in Denver."

There. He'd finally told her. He reached inside his hat and pulled out Tom Caldwell's letter. Handing it to her, he waited patiently while she read it through. Twice. Then, she folded the pages, put them inside the envelope and handed it back to him. The only betrayal of her apparent calm was that her hand visibly trembled.

"So you're definitely going to leave again," she said. It was a statement, not a question.

"I haven't decided yet."

She folded her arms, as if she were cold. Since she was wearing her cape and the barn was quite warm, he doubted that.

"But you must be seriously considering accepting the offer or you wouldn't have shown me the letter," she said.

She was upset. He knew it instinctively. He could tell by the way her spine stiffened and she lifted her chin slightly higher in the air. Given the circumstances, he couldn't blame her.

"*Ja*, my logic tells me the work in Denver would give me more opportunities than staying here. But I love my life here too. I love the farm work, I love my *familye* and I love…"

He shook his head, wondering what he was about to say. He wasn't sure. A muddle of thoughts filled his mind. He was still missing Shannon more than he could say, but she was gone. Now, he was here with Lizzie.

"What about your faith?" she asked.

He nodded and placed a hand over his chest. "*Ja*, I still have it here in my heart."

She quirked one eyebrow at him. "Do you? When

you go back to Denver, how can you live your faith when you are apart from your *familye* and never join us at church? Just like a bright coal that is pulled away from the flames of a fire, you would eventually lose the warmth of your faith."

He caught a tone of reservation in her voice. But deep inside, he believed in *Gott*. His faith was all that had carried him through after Shannon had passed away. Before he could say so, Lizzie quoted an old Amish saying.

"If you must doubt, then doubt your doubts, not your beliefs," she said.

He heard the conviction in her voice, but no judgment. Her face looked passive, her voice so composed…just another one of her good qualities. Except when they had played volleyball or baseball, he couldn't remember hearing her raise her voice. And he wasn't sure why he'd told her about the offer or what else he expected her to say. Of course she wouldn't want him to leave. Her faith was strong and she believed families should stay together.

"You always were so straightforward and sensible," he said.

"Is that wrong? What else do you want me to say?" she asked.

He hung his head. "I don't know. On the one hand, I wish you'd tell me it's okay to live among the *Englisch*. That I'm still a *gut* man and acceptable to the Lord if I return to Denver. But a part of me also wishes you'd yell and scream at me and tell me that you want me to stay here with my *familye* and…"

You.

Now where had that thought come from? He wasn't sure.

"*Ach*, of course I want you to stay here. We are your people. You belong here. There, I've said it. But it didn't make you feel any better, did it?"

No, it didn't. And he realized the problem wasn't with his faith, his *familye*, or his work as a paramedic. The problem was with him. He loved both worlds, but hadn't accepted himself so that he could decide where he wanted to be. Where he truly felt he belonged and where the Lord wanted him to live.

"You…you won't mention this to my *mudder* or *vadder* or anyone else, will you? It would only upset them," he said.

A deep, wrenching sadness filled her eyes and he thought for a moment that she was going to cry. "*Ne*, I won't tell a soul. But, Eli, keeping it a secret will only delay the inevitable. What do you want? Where do you want to be? Unfortunately, you can't choose both lives."

He couldn't answer. He honestly didn't know.

"I wish you felt a firm conviction of who you are and where you ought to be. Because once you know that deep inside, there will be no turning back and you will feel a deep, abiding joy and confidence in your life. I'll pray that you find that peace very soon."

She turned and left as quietly as she had come. He stared after her for a very long time, pondering her words. Wishing he could know for a certainty where he belonged. But no answers came.

Chapter Eleven

"I don't want to do it. I tell you, I don't need to exercise."

Eli heard the irritable words as he entered the back door to the kitchen and set a pail of milk on the table. Morning sunbeams glinted off the snow-covered fields and sprayed a ray of light through the window over the stainless steel sink. The little girls' happy voices carried from upstairs. Apparently they didn't have school today so the teacher could attend some meetings.

Across the countertops and table, a variety of large and small plastic bowls, brown bottles, powders, spatulas and long wooden molds covered with freezer paper had been set out in an orderly fashion. Eli recognized the molds as the same type his mother used to make soap and he figured that was Lizzie's planned work for the day. But she wasn't in here now.

"Leave me alone, I say." Jeremiah's unmistakable curt voice came from the living area.

"But, *Daed*, the doctor said you must do these exercises twice each day so you can regain your strength." Lizzie's pleading explanation was filled with frustration.

Knowing that Jeremiah didn't want him around, Eli turned toward the door. Like a coward, he planned to flee to the barn.

"And I'm not buying dumbbells either. I've lived my whole life without lifting weights. It's a bunch of foolishness, if you ask me."

"But, *Daed*, you've been in bed for weeks already. You need to move your muscles."

Eli paused at the back door, his hand on the knob. No, he was not going to interfere. This wasn't his business. He should leave them alone and return to his chores.

"*Daed*…please."

That did it. Turning, Eli walked into the living room. He had taken a couple of classes on physical therapy and understood the process. He could help, if Jeremiah and Lizzie would let him. If there was any way he could help ease Lizzie's frustration, he had to try.

Jeremiah was sitting upright on the bed, his legs extended on top of the covers with his casted leg cradled by two pillows. Except for his missing hat and bare feet, the man was fully dressed for the day. A breakfast tray, basin of water, toothbrush and shaving implements rested on the coffee table nearby, along with a towel and comb. Eli couldn't help thinking Lizzie was taking good care of her father.

Clearing his voice, he stepped near. "Can I help?"

Lizzie whirled around and the papers she was holding fluttered to the wood floor. Eli saw that they were covered with pictures, showing how to correctly perform a number of simple exercises.

"Eli! *Guder mariye*," she said as she quickly gathered up the pages.

He nodded respectfully, noticing her ruffled expression. *"Guder mariye."*

"What do you want?" Jeremiah looked away, as if dismissing him.

Since Eli had dealt with obstinate patients before, he didn't feel intimidated one bit. And knowing how hard Lizzie was trying to help her father, Eli decided to be blunt.

"I want to offer my services."

Jeremiah glared. "What are you talking about? You're already running my farm."

Resigning himself to being patient, Eli smiled tolerantly. "That's not what I mean. I'm trained and have worked with physical therapy patients before."

"You…you have?" Lizzie said, her eyes filled with startled wonder.

He nodded. *"Ja,* when I was trying to decide what field I wanted to go into, I took some extra classes. I thought perhaps I could help your *vadder* with his exercises."

"I don't need to exercise, nor do I need your help," Jeremiah replied, his tone a low rumble.

Hmm. Maybe Eli should try a different approach.

"Of course you need to exercise. As Lizzie pointed out, it'll strengthen your body. Without it, your muscles will atrophy from lack of use. Once you're able to get up and walk again, you won't be able to do the work. You'll be weak and winded. And then I'll have to stay here on your farm even longer."

Ah! That did the trick. Jeremiah's eyes widened and he stared at Eli with open shock.

Eli hated to use such tactics, but knew it was the only way to get through to Jeremiah. It couldn't be easy for a hardworking man like Jeremiah to sit around idle all day, dependent on the help of a man he didn't even like to keep the farm running. Up until the accident, he had led a vital, busy, self-sufficient life. No wonder he was so irritable.

Releasing a cantankerous sigh, Jeremiah pursed his lips together. "*Ach*, all right. Let's get on with it then."

Lizzie smiled and threw an expression of gratitude in Eli's direction. In her eyes, he could see that she understood what he'd just done. Reverse psychology, of sorts. But if it got Jeremiah to cooperate, then it was worth the effort.

"Do you have some unopened soup cans that weigh about one pound each?" Eli asked Lizzie.

"*Ja*, in the cupboard." Without asking what they were for, she hurried into the kitchen and soon returned with two cans of soup. She handed them to Eli, then stepped back.

Jeremiah eyed the cans with a belligerent scowl. "What are you gonna do with those?"

"Since you don't have any one- or two-pound dumbbells, you can lift cans of soup to exercise your arms. It's cheaper and just as effective…unless you're already too weak to lift them," Eli added, trying to needle Jeremiah into doing the exercises.

"Humph! Of course I can do it," Jeremiah said.

Eli thought he heard a muffled laugh coming from Lizzie, but didn't look her way. Jeremiah murmured something about looking silly lifting soup cans that Eli chose to ignore.

"Can you do this?" Eli proceeded to clasp a can in

each hand and do several biceps curls. Then he handed the cans over to Jeremiah.

Conscious of Lizzie watching with interest, Eli waited as Jeremiah did the curls.

"That is *gut*, but what about doing it this way?" Taking the cans, Eli showed Jeremiah a variation of curls that would exercise different muscles in his neck, shoulders, arms and back.

"*Ja*, I can do all of them." Jeremiah took the cans and mimicked Eli in perfect fashion.

"That is very *gut*. But slow down just a bit and concentrate on working your muscles. Feel your movements and make them worth the effort," Eli encouraged.

Jeremiah did as asked and Eli counted out two sets of eight repetitions before they switched to a different exercise.

"I heard your doctor tell Lizzie that he wants you to aim for full weight bearing on your leg within three weeks. In order to do that, you should exercise your good leg too," Eli said.

He didn't want to confess that, while Lizzie was helping Jeremiah pack for his trip home, Eli had spoken with Dr. McGann out in the reception room at the hospital. Eli hadn't expected to help Jeremiah with his exercises, but he was naturally curious and so he'd educated himself on what the man needed to do.

When he glanced Lizzie's way, Eli discovered that she had vacated the room. The subtle sounds of tap water running in the kitchen and dishes clanking told him she was doing her morning chores. He continued to work with Jeremiah, coaxing the older man to lay flat so he could lift, push and stretch his healthy leg.

Soon, they'd completed the variety of tasks the doctor had recommended.

"There, you're all done for the morning. But you need to do the same exercises this afternoon. It wasn't so hard, was it?" Eli asked.

"*Ne*, it wasn't hard," Jeremiah responded.

But Eli knew the man was covering the exhaustion he felt. Jeremiah's breathing sounded heavy and his arms trembled as he tried to do extra repetitions of the exercises. Even just a few weeks of inactivity had left his body weaker, but Eli doubted the man would ever confess that out loud. At least, not to him.

"Tomorrow, try to do an extra set of each exercise. You'll soon find that the work gets easier and you'll be able to do more each day." Ignoring Jeremiah's cloudy frown, Eli spoke in a cheery, optimistic tone.

"*Ja*, I will do as you say," Jeremiah said.

Pleased by this admission, Eli turned toward the kitchen. "And now, I had better get on with my work. Send one of the *maed* for me if you need anything at all."

"I won't need anything from you," Jeremiah said.

Pretending not to notice the man's deep scowl, Eli hid a smile as he walked out of the room. As he entered the kitchen and saw Lizzie standing in front of the counter, he felt suddenly light of heart. The ties of her *kapp* hung loose against her shoulders and he was tempted to tug playfully on them. No, he better not. She was still on edge around him. But he had to admit it felt great to be needed.

Wearing goggles and a face mask, Lizzie set the heavy plastic bowl on the battery-operated scale and measured out the distilled water. When she finished, she reached for the jar of sodium hydroxide, or lye as it was commonly called.

As he spoke to her father, the sound of Eli's deep voice reached her from the living room. She paused a moment, trying to hear his words.

Glancing at the new recipe Abby had given her, she read through the list of ingredients again. Now where was she?

Eli's laughter caused her to glance toward the door. With a sigh, she picked up the recipe one more time. Glancing at the bowl of water, she shook her head in disgust. She'd barely started and had already made a huge mistake. She wanted to double this batch of soap, which meant she needed more distilled water. Why couldn't she seem to concentrate today?

Setting aside the lye, she picked up the water jug and added the proper amount to the bowl. She was too distracted by her father and Eli. Determined to focus on her work, she again reached for the lye. Removing the lid, she shook the container to get the white chips to fall out into the bowl.

"Lizzie?"

She jerked, splashing lye chips into the water. The caustic liquid spattered her hands and arms and she dropped the container of chips. Of all the foolish things to do…she'd forgotten to put on her rubber gloves.

Thankfully, the lye container thudded onto the counter top rather than spilling across the floor. The last thing she wanted was to clean up a big lye spill. But she flinched in pain as the corrosive alkaline solution burned her bare flesh.

"Ouch!" she cried.

Before she knew what was happening, she found herself leaning over the sink. A gush of fresh water rushed over her hands from the tap.

She stared at the stream for several moments, shocked by what had happened. Then, she looked up at Eli. He stood close, his face only a breath away. He held her hands, his touch gentle but firm.

"Is that better?" he asked.

"Um, *ja*, it is…"

She couldn't finish, barely able to gather her thoughts. Their gazes met and she couldn't have moved away to save her life. She felt locked there, held prisoner by her own suppressed longings. As if time stood still and he had never left Riverton and nothing bad had ever happened between them.

"Does it still hurt?" he asked, his voice slightly husky.

"What…?"

He repeated the question.

She blinked, trying to remember where she was. Trying to think. "*Ne*, I think it's fine now."

"Do you have some vinegar?" he asked.

"*Ja*." But she didn't move.

"Where is it? It'll help neutralize the lye and stop the burning."

"*Ach*, of course."

With water dripping down her arms, she reached into a cupboard and took out a bottle. Before she could act, he removed it from her hand and unscrewed the lid. He reached for a hand towel and tipped the bottle so that it saturated the fabric. Then he pressed it against the myriad of small splotches on her skin where the lye had burned her. Her nose twitched at the pungent scent of vinegar, but she felt instant relief.

Looking up, she found his lips were but a space away from hers. She felt his warm breath tickle her cheek. Felt the warmth of his fingers against her skin. It happened again. That magnetic attraction she'd thought was long dead.

"Lizzie-bee," he whispered, drawing nearer.

He kissed her. A soft, gentle caress that filled her with a yearning she had forgotten years ago. She closed her eyes and let herself go...

"Lizzie, *Daed* needs another pillow."

They jerked apart as Marty bounced into the kitchen.

Lizzie flinched and turned aside, clasping the dish towel with her hands. As Eli turned off the water faucet, she snuck a worried glance over at Marty, relieved to note that the girl didn't seem to notice anything wrong. But Lizzie still felt the strong emotions buzzing between her and Eli. Had the moment affected him as much as it had her?

"Of course. I'll get one right now," she said, swiveling toward the door.

This was a good excuse to get out of here right now. She stole a glance at Eli, trying to see his face and assess his mood. He ducked his head as he dried his own hands on the discarded towel, seeming completely composed. And it was just as well. After all, he was considering another job in Denver. He was planning to leave again. He had loved Shannon and didn't want her. Deep in her heart, Lizzie had always known he wouldn't stay. That the call of the *Englisch* world was too strong for him to resist. But she'd hoped and prayed he might find life in Riverton too compelling to leave.

Her decision not to let herself fall in love with him again had been wise. And yet, moments like this reminded her of how much they'd once cared for one another. It would be so easy to let down her guard and...

No! She mustn't think that way. Eli was leaving and that was that.

As she walked out of the kitchen, she didn't look back to see if Eli was watching her. But she didn't have to. She could feel his eyes on her just as surely as she lived.

Chapter Twelve

Eli lifted the full bucket of milk and moved it carefully out from beneath the Holstein. The cow stamped a foot and gave a low *moo*. A little of the frothy milk sloshed over the brim and Eli steadied his hold on the handle. He shouldn't have filled the bucket so full, but he'd been thinking about what had happened yesterday with Lizzie. He never should have kissed her. Never should have gotten so close to her. Not only was he still heartsick over losing Shannon, but he was seriously considering leaving soon. So, what had he been thinking?

Bending over one of the tall canisters, he poured the milk inside. At a sound in the doorway, he looked up, surprised to see Lizzie standing there. After what had happened between them, he would have thought she would avoid him like the plague. He blinked, thinking she was his imagination playing tricks on his mind. But no. She stood in front of the open doorway, her slender body silhouetted by morning sunlight.

"Lizzie-bee," he whispered her name, or at least he thought he did. He wasn't sure.

She wore a light blue dress, her black apron and white *kapp* both crisp and perfectly starched. He caught a brief whiff of her scent, a subtle mixture of cinnamon and vanilla. He wasn't surprised. She was always baking something delicious to eat.

"Eli," she said.

"Lizzie," he spoke at the same time.

They both laughed with embarrassment.

After setting the bucket on the ground, he stood up straight. "Sorry. You go first."

She waved a hand in the air. "*Ne*, tell me what you wanted to say. My issue will probably take longer to discuss."

Folding her hands together in front of her, she waited with a firm, but serene expression. He never should have kissed her. Now, he felt like a heel. He'd simply forgotten himself in the moment. But he didn't want Lizzie to think he was using her. She already thought he was too worldly, too filled with pride. He'd be mortified if she thought he was taking advantage of her. But how could he explain what he'd done when he didn't understand it himself?

"I… I'm sorry for what happened yesterday. So very sorry. I've regretted it ever since and wanted you to know how bad I feel…"

She stiffened, then shook her head emphatically. "I'm sorry you regret it, but you're right. It was an accident. It never should have happened."

She turned away and he hurried to clasp her arm. He didn't want to drive her away. Trying to be gentle, he pulled her back around.

"*Ne*, Lizzie. I… I didn't mean it like that. I don't

really regret our kiss. *Ach*, I do, but I don't. It's just that…"

"There's no need for you to explain. We won't discuss it ever again. Please just let it drop now."

He opened his mouth to say something more. Something that didn't sound so ridiculous. But she didn't give him the chance.

"I have a small request, if you wouldn't mind." She took a step back, her hands fluttering nervously for a moment.

He stared at her in confusion. That was it? They weren't going to discuss the kiss? She'd barely let him apologize. There was more he wanted to say. To clarify and try to help her understand. After all, she deserved an explanation. But since he didn't know what to say, maybe dropping the subject was for the best.

"What is it? Anything you need. Just name it," he said.

Okay, maybe he was overcompensating now. But he realized that he'd do almost anything for this woman. Anything at all. She'd earned his admiration and respect and he considered her to be one of the best people he'd ever been privileged to know.

"I would like to attend the quilting frolic over at Naomi's farm this morning. We will be working on some new baby quilts for Abby. The *maed* would like to go with me, to play with the other *kinder*." Her voice sounded hesitant, as if she feared he might think her desires were foolish or frivolous.

He nodded, delighted that she was telling him about a normal, mundane event. "*Ja*, you absolutely should go. It would be *gut* for you to get out of here for a while. The roads are clear and you should have no problems driving the buggy."

After all, tending to the demanding needs of a grumpy man like Jeremiah couldn't be easy all the time. It might do both Lizzie and the girls good to get out and have a little fun for once.

She frowned. "*Ach*, I have one problem, though."

His hearing perked up at that. Lizzie was actually confiding in him, seeking his advice. It was like they were real friends again. He hoped.

He stood close, looking down at her sweet face. "What is it?"

"While I'm gone, would you mind checking in on *Daed* now and then? I've prepared a lunch for both of you and put it in the cooler. When the time comes, if you wouldn't mind getting it out for him and, you know, seeing to his other needs, I'd greatly appreciate it." She shrugged, her cheeks flushing a pretty shade of pink.

Without asking for more details, he understood her meaning. "Of course. I'd be happy to look in on Jeremiah from time to time. I'm sure I can help him with anything he might need. And it might be fun to eat lunch with him today."

A doubtful frown pulled at her lips and he laughed. "Don't worry. We will both be just fine."

She showed a smile so bright that it made his throat ache.

"*Danke*, that would be great. But I should warn you. He's not happy about being alone for most of the day. He has *The Budget* newspaper and plenty of other reading material close at hand, but he may be a bit grouchy with you. I think he's got cabin fever something fierce. Are you sure you're up to spending time with him throughout the day?"

Her eyes were so wide and hopeful that he wouldn't have had the heart to deny her, even if he was so inclined. Which he wasn't.

"*Ja*, we'll be fine. You leave Jeremiah to me." He smiled, trying to convey a self-confidence he wasn't sure he really felt. He knew Jeremiah didn't like him anymore, but was determined to win him over. Maybe this was just what they needed.

"Will you be leaving soon?" he asked.

She nodded. "As soon as the *maed* are ready. They've just finished breakfast and are brushing their teeth now."

"*Gut*. I'll get the horse and buggy hitched up and bring them outside for you," he offered.

"*Danke*."

She turned and walked away, a happy bounce in her stride. She didn't look back at him. He knew because he stared after her to see if she would. And though it made no sense to him, he couldn't help feeling a tad disappointed that she didn't.

An hour later, Eli reached a stopping point in his work and decided to check on Jeremiah. He fidgeted with his hat, feeling suddenly more wary than normal. In spite of speaking with Lizzie's father almost every day, Eli had yet to be alone with him. Since he'd returned from the hospital, there'd always been someone else in the room with them. Lizzie or one of her sisters. With someone else always around, there had been no opportunity for them to discuss that Jeremiah was the one who had returned Eli's letters.

Opening the back door to the kitchen, Eli stepped inside. He let the screen door clap closed behind him, purposefully alerting Jeremiah that he was here. Then he thought better of it. What if the man was napping?

"Hallo," Eli called to the house.

He stepped into the living room, automatically glancing toward the bed. Jeremiah sat reclining against a pile of pillows, a newspaper resting beside him on the mattress. His left fingers still held the page. It looked as if he'd just lowered it there. He wore a pair of black reading glasses and peered at Eli from over the narrow frames.

"Did you need something?" Jeremiah asked, his voice still filled with a disapproving curtness.

"Ne, I just wanted to check on you, to see how you're doing." Eli forced himself to put a smile in his voice. After all, this man wasn't his enemy and he wished they'd never had any hostility between them.

"I'm doing fine." Jeremiah picked the newspaper up again, as if brushing Eli aside.

"Would you like your lunch now? It's about that time. Are you hungry yet?" Eli pressed.

Because he'd eaten so early that morning, Eli was famished and ready for the yummy meal Lizzie had prepared for them.

Jeremiah again lowered the paper to his lap and removed his glasses, setting them on top of a pile of magazines that rested beside him. He gazed at Eli for a few moments, his bushy eyebrows lifted in consideration.

"Ja, I could eat now. Why don't you go see what Lizzie prepared for us?"

Really? That wasn't so hard.

Turning, Eli returned to the kitchen. He went to

the gas-powered refrigerator and opened the door, leaning down so he could peer inside. Sitting on the middle rack, he found two plates covered with plastic wrap. They each contained sandwiches made with thin slices of homemade bread and moist, thick cuts of meatloaf…probably leftover from last night's supper. A note lay atop a shoofly pie that said: *Enjoy*! As he got the plates out along with a pitcher of chilled milk, Eli's mouth watered in anticipation. He never doubted Lizzie's cooking skills. She would make some man an excellent wife.

He frowned. For some crazy reason, he didn't like the thought of her marrying someone else. And because of his relationship with Shannon, that didn't seem right.

He poured the milk and carried a tray of the food into the living room. As he set it beside Jeremiah, he didn't feel as nervous as before. That changed the moment he sat in a chair next to the elder man and took a bite of his sandwich.

"*Ach*, what are your plans for the future?" Jeremiah asked.

Eli coughed and took a quick swallow of milk to clear his throat.

"Um, I plan to live and work just as before," he said.

Jeremiah took a slow bite, chewed for a moment, then swallowed. During the entire time, his gaze never wavered from Eli. "Here in Riverton? Or will you return to Denver?"

Eli blinked, wondering if Lizzie had told her father about the job offer. He doubted it—she had said she would keep his secret. Until he was baptized into their faith, everyone in the *Gmay* was wondering if he would stay or go. For most everyone, Eli was able to brush aside their blunt questions. But something about Jeremiah's piercing gaze seemed to look deep inside of him for the truth. Because he'd always respected this man and because he was Lizzie's father, Eli couldn't lie to him. But how could he admit he didn't know for sure what he would do?

"I plan to stay."

Since he hadn't decided if he wanted to leave, he thought that was an honest enough response.

"*Gut.* I've seen the way you look at my *dochder*, and I'll admit I've been concerned."

What? The way he looked at Lizzie?

Eli tilted his head to the side. "I don't understand. I don't look any special way at her," Eli said, feeling totally confused.

Jeremiah snorted, then took another bite of food, chewed calmly and swallowed before responding. "I don't want you to hurt her again the way you did last time you left. Nor do I want her to run away with you. You sent her letters before. I imagine they asked for her to join you in Denver."

So. Here it was. The topic had turned around to the letters. Eli knew it would. Eventually. And he couldn't deny that he *had* asked Lizzie to come to him in those letters.

"I didn't run away. I just left," Eli said.

One of Jeremiah's bushy eyebrows shot up. "Is there a difference?"

"I think so. But are you referring to the letters I wrote to Lizzie, which you returned to me? Unopened? Without even telling her about them?"

Jeremiah met Eli's gaze without a single drop of shame in his eyes.

"*Ja*, those would be the ones. I don't want you to do that again. It would hurt Lizzie too much. She is a gut *maedel* and deserves better from her fiancé."

"We were only fourteen years old when I asked her to marry me."

"So? Why does it matter how old you were? Are you a man of your word or not?" Jeremiah paused, waiting for a response that didn't come.

Once again, Eli felt rotten inside. The foolishness of his youth seemed to keep haunting him.

"I regret hurting her more than I can say. When she didn't write back to me, I assumed she no longer wanted me and our engagement was broken," Eli said.

Jeremiah didn't respond to that. He simply looked at Eli with that calm, unemotional expression of his. Finally, he picked up his fork and took a big bite of pie.

"I don't regret returning your letters and I'd do it again if the situation was the same," Jeremiah said.

Eli flinched at these words. He thought their conversation was over, but apparently not.

"I do regret that my *dochder* got hurt when you ran away to the *Englisch* world," Jeremiah continued. "I hope you've figured out who you are by now. Because no amount of education, no career or accolades of men, no wealth or worldly success can ever compensate for failure in your own home. Every man must live with the man he makes of himself. As you prepare for your future, I hope you'll never forget that. Especially where my *dochder* is concerned."

Every man must live with the man he makes of himself.

Eli hesitated, these words playing over and over in his mind. Since it was an old Amish saying, he'd heard it many times from his own father. But never before had it struck him with such powerful force. Such meaning.

He thought about the past, present and future, and wanted more than anything to be content with the man he became at the end of his life. To be able to meet the Lord without shame. To know he'd done his absolute best and kept trying even when he failed. To have as few regrets in his life as he could possibly make. But what did that have to do with Lizzie? They were no longer engaged and his future no longer included her.

Or did it?

Chapter Thirteen

Over the next few weeks, Lizzie and her *familye* settled into a routine. In the mornings and early after-
noons, Jeremiah grudgingly accepted Eli's help with
the simple exercises the doctor had recommended.
When they drove into town to visit Dr. McGann, he
was more than pleased by Jeremiah's progress.

Each evening, before he went home, Eli would come
into the house to sit and talk with Jeremiah about his
work for the following day. No longer did Lizzie's father speak to Eli with a gruff, disapproving voice, although he was still reserved around the younger man.

On this particular afternoon, the wind and a lashing
rain buffeted the house, but Lizzie felt warm and cozy
inside. Because of the stormy weather, she had dried
the laundry on racks set up in the living room. As she
folded each piece and laid it inside the wicker basket,
she couldn't help eavesdropping on the men's low conversation. The little girls sat on the couch nearby, reading quietly to one another. Outside, dark clouds filled
the sky. The rain had slowed to a smattering that hit
the windowpanes. Lizzie glanced that way, grateful to

be inside. As she lit a kerosene lamp and set it nearby on a table so the children could see more easily, she thought the moment seemed so tranquil. So relaxed and normal, but it wasn't. Not for Lizzie.

No matter how many days passed, she couldn't forget the kiss she'd shared with Eli. Every time she saw him, she became nervous and quivery inside. When she thought of how much he must still love Shannon, she felt completely confused. Why had he kissed her? Had he forgotten who she was? But more than that, why had she kissed him back?

"What about the disc plow? Have you sharpened the blades yet?" Jeremiah asked Eli.

The older man sat upright on his bed with several pillows to support his back. Eli sat nearby in a hard chair.

"*Ja*, I took care of that as soon as Lizzie and I finished baling and putting the hay away," came Eli's even reply.

"And the baler...does it need any maintenance?"

Eli shook his head. "*Ne*, but I cleaned it out *gut* and got it ready for next season. The harness required mending and I replaced several buckles. The *maed* helped me."

Jeremiah glanced at his younger daughters, approval shining in his eyes.

"The barn roof also needed a few repairs. I found your extra shingles and did the work before the storms hit," Eli said.

"*Gut, gut.* Tomorrow, I'd like you to check the fence again, if the weather isn't too bad. I don't want any of the livestock to get out."

"I will do so," Eli confirmed.

Hefting the laundry basket, Lizzie climbed the stairs. She felt a mixture of gratitude and uncertainty. Eli had become immersed in their lives, almost as if he was a part of their *familye*. And he wasn't.

He acted as if he wanted to stay in Riverton, but Lizzie knew he was still drawn to worldly pursuits. If only he could find his *Gelassenheit* and accept that he was born to be an Amish man. She wondered how his leaving might impact his parents and the rest of the *Gmay*.

And her.

Thinking about his eventual departure made her heart pound harder. She told herself it was because she feared for his salvation. Her faith would allow nothing less. She truly believed that, if he turned his back on their faith and left Riverton, his soul would be in jeopardy. And no matter how many times she told herself it was his choice, she still longed for a way to convince him to stay.

Inside the children's room, she placed their folded clothes tidily in their dressers. She crossed the hall to her room and looked up. A shoebox she did not recognize sat on top of her chest of drawers.

Wondering what it was, she set the laundry basket on the floor, then lifted the lid to the box. A gasp tore from her throat and she stepped back, covering her lips with the fingertips of one hand. Her thoughts scattered. Inside, tied together with a bit of string, was a hefty stack of sealed letters. Each one was addressed to her, the postmark from Denver several years earlier. Without asking, she knew these were Eli's letters. The ones her father had returned.

Reaching inside, she lifted out the stack, then closed

the door to give herself more privacy. The bed bounced gently as she sat on one corner. Resting the pile of letters in her lap, she stared at them for at least five minutes. Her body trembled when she finally untied the string. She withdrew the first letter, but her shaking hands immediately dropped it to the floor. Bending at the waist, she picked it up. What was the matter with her? After so many years, these letters should make no difference in her life. They shouldn't matter. But they did.

Obviously, Eli had put the letters here for her to find. Maybe she should return them to him, or burn them and forget they ever existed.

The envelopes had been arranged in chronological order. She told herself that, if she didn't read them, nothing in her life would change. She could go on the way she was, filled with heartbreak and doubt. And that's when she realized how comfortable she'd become with those two emotions as her constant companions.

She felt compelled to read. She had to know what Eli had said to her. The letters were a part of her somehow. A part of her life—and Eli's life—that she'd missed because her father had withheld them from her.

She slid her finger beneath the flap of the first envelope. As she pulled out the crisp pages and unfolded them, she took a deep breath, trying to settle her nerves. She immediately recognized Eli's scrawling handwriting. Her gaze scanned the words, a hard lump as big as a boulder lodging in her throat. Eli conveyed his regrets over leaving her without saying goodbye. He expressed his love for her and a wish that she would join him in Denver. He still wanted to marry her, if she wanted him. He would await her reply…a response that never came.

One by one, Lizzie read the pile of letters, dazed by Eli's explanations of his fierce desire for a college education and skeptical of his declarations of love for her. Toward the end, he conveyed the deep sense of loss he felt when she didn't write back, and returned his letters unopened. In between, he discussed his schooling and work as a waiter in a restaurant to make ends meet. He looked mature for his age and had rented a studio apartment that was small but clean and had room for her. Every day, he walked to school, sitting in classes that tantalized his intellect and convinced him more and more of an eternal *Gott* who loved all his children unconditionally. Instead of weakening his faith, his education had strengthened his beliefs. Several times, he asked why she wouldn't write to him. He begged her to reconsider and join him in his *Englisch* life.

To marry him.

And then the final letter. Lizzie maintained her composure as she read Eli's deep sense of sorrow because he realized he'd lost her for good. He said he understood why she hadn't written him. That their breakup was his fault and he couldn't blame her for not wanting a life with him outside of the *Gmay*. She deserved a man of faith who never questioned their leaders or *Gott*'s will for them. It was time for them both to move on.

And that was the end.

Folding the last letter, Lizzie added it to the stack and retied the string. She put the letters back in their box and settled the lid over the top of them. Fearing her father or sisters might find and read them, she slid them far beneath her bed where they wouldn't be discovered easily.

So, now she knew. She'd finally read Eli's letters. His words were highly personal and gave her a new insight into who he really was inside. And for the first time since she'd known him, she finally understood his desire to learn new things. And she was surprised to find that it didn't make her angry anymore. Because she'd loved him so much, she couldn't condemn him. She had to let him choose for himself, no matter how much it hurt her.

Taking a deep, settling breath, she smoothed her skirt and apron. A quick glance in the tiny mirror on her nightstand caused her to tidy her hair and adjust her *kapp*. Chores were waiting. She had to go on with her life. She couldn't while away the day by sulking here in her room. She had to go downstairs and tend to her father and sisters. She had to be strong and resolute. Firm in her faith and her place in the world.

She took a step toward the door. She clutched the knob, but couldn't make it turn so she could leave. She stared at the oak panel, her vision blurring. Something gave way inside of her and she burst into deep, trembling sobs.

It was time to go. The rain had finally stopped, the evening air filled with the crisp scent of damp sage. Eli had finished his work and harnessed his horse to the buggy, but couldn't seem to get inside and drive away. Instead, he stood at the barn doors, gazing out at the damp farmyard. It was already dark with not even the stars or moon to light his way home. Without being able to see them, he knew the sky was filled with heavy, black clouds.

For the sake of safety, he should get on the road now, before it got any later. *Mamm* and *Daed* were expecting him for supper. But he hesitated, wondering if Lizzie had read the letters he'd left in her room. Wondering if she might come out to speak with him about them. He'd watched her go upstairs and knew she must have found them.

As he surveyed the house, the lights in the kitchen brightened and he knew she must be inside, preparing supper for her *familye*. Soon, Jeremiah would be up and walking again. His leg would continue to heal and he wouldn't need Eli's help on the farm anymore. Eli could leave, if he chose to do so. He could return to Denver and his old life there. No Shannon or Lizzie to welcome him. No love to share.

Completely alone.

Lizzie wasn't coming out to the barn. His stomach rumbled and he realized it was time to eat. His parents would be worried if he didn't arrive soon. Lizzie was occupied elsewhere. She probably didn't care about the letters now. He wasn't sure what he had expected. That she would read them and come running into his arms to declare that she still loved him? That she wanted to marry him and raise a *familye* with him here in Riverton? That wasn't what he wanted, was it? He was still in love with Shannon. Right?

He snorted and turned away, returning to his buggy. He'd always been so firm in what he wanted out of life. So convinced that the *Englisch* life was best for him. But now, he felt nothing but conflict. He was even starting to doubt his love for Shannon. Sometimes, he couldn't remember her face. All he could remember was Lizzie. And that wasn't right. No, it couldn't be.

Pulling on his warm gloves, he led the horse out into the yard and secured the barn doors. He climbed into his buggy seat and took hold of the lead lines.

"Schritt!" he called.

The horse stepped forward, pulling the buggy through puddles of water along the dirt road.

Eli figured his letters to Lizzie were too little, too late. In the time since he had written them, he'd fallen in love with someone else. It still hurt like a knife to his heart every time he thought about losing Shannon. But lately, he couldn't remember the shape of her eyes, or the contour of her chin. Whenever he thought about her, his thoughts turned to Lizzie. Which was foolish because she didn't care for him anymore. Not romantically, anyway. They'd both moved on with their lives. And yet, he couldn't help wishing…

He was being stupid! He had no idea why he'd kissed her. He'd been so embarrassed by what he'd done. So ashamed.

He turned the buggy onto the county road, pulling over to the shoulder. The horse trotted forward, eager to get home.

Every time Lizzie was in the room with him, Eli felt a deeper sense of guilt. Kissing her had been wrong on so many levels. His lapse in judgment hadn't been fair to either of them. It might lead her to believe there could be something between them again. That he still loved her the way he used to. And he didn't. Did he?

He remembered all the times when he'd thought Lizzie was rejecting his letters because she was disappointed in him. He thought she had returned them all to him. Because he'd turned his back on his faith and their love. And all that time, she hadn't even known that he had written to her. From her perspective, she must have thought he'd abandoned her completely, without any explanation. That he'd broken all his promises to her. That he'd chosen the world over her. And that wasn't true. He'd begged her to join him— had wanted to share the world with her. But that had been a foolish dream. Lizzie had never wanted a life anywhere other than here.

He shook his head. The letter from Tom Caldwell was still folded inside his hat. He hadn't responded to the job offer yet. For the time being, Lizzie's *familye* still needed his help. But soon, Jeremiah would be back on his feet. So, what was holding Eli back? He wasn't sure, but knew he'd have to make a decision soon. And he'd need to speak to Lizzie as well. To tell her he was deeply, genuinely sorry for how things had not worked out between them. She deserved that apology and so much more. He only hoped she could find it in her heart to forgive him.

Chapter Fourteen

The day of Church Sunday was a pleasant surprise. The Sangre de Cristo Mountains were coated with snow, but down in the valley everything had melted off the roads and fields. The sun gleamed bright and surprisingly warm in the morning sky. Not bad, considering they were only a week away from Thanksgiving. As Lizzie hurried to gather the eggs, she thought it most fitting for the *Gmay*'s semiannual Communion meeting. It should be a day of enlightenment and confidence in the Lord. But for herself, she still felt overshadowed by qualms.

"Lizzie?"

She turned. Eli stood just beyond the open doorway, his dark hair shining against his sun-bronzed face. Wearing his best clothes, he held his hat in his hands. Seeing him brought a quick leap of excitement to her chest, but she tried to squelch it. She'd avoided him for a long time now. Perhaps today of all days, it was time to speak with him and let go of her harsh feelings. Instead of nursing her own broken heart, she should think about other people for a change…starting with Eli.

Carrying the wire basket filled with eggs, she stepped outside and latched the door of the chicken coop. Then, she looked up into his eyes.

"*Guder mariye*, Eli. *Wie bischt du heit?*"

"I am *gut*, but I am worried about you," he said.

She took a deep inhale of the crisp air and let it go, reminding herself to remain calm. To trust in the Lord. And to forgive.

"Why would you be worried about me?" she asked, thinking she knew the answer, but not quite sure.

He looked at the ground, his chiseled profile so handsome that she almost reached out to touch his cheek. Almost.

"I… I owe you an apology," he said.

Yes, he did, but she didn't say that.

"For what?" she said instead.

His gaze met hers and in his eyes, she saw deep remorse there. "For so many things. For kissing you. For leaving all those years ago without saying goodbye in person. For not coming to see you when you didn't respond to my letters. For breaking off our engagement. For being a stupid, foolish kid. I was young and *dumm* and wanted a *rumspringa*."

She showed a sad little smile. "*Ach*, then you got what you wanted."

"*Ja*, but I regret putting myself first and not thinking about how my leaving might affect you and my *eldre*. I'm sorry for the pain I caused. I can't look back and regret my life, but I do deeply regret hurting you, both now and in the past."

Oh, did he have to say that?

"*Es tut mir leid*. Can you please forgive me for what I did?" he continued.

Here it was. The moment she'd been dreading. Forgiveness was a requirement of her faith. If she truly believed in Christ and the Atonement, then she must pardon Eli for any wrongs he'd done to her. Repentance wasn't just for her. It was for others as well. But still she hesitated, her pulse quickening as she pondered what to say. And yet, there was really only one response she could give.

"Of course I forgive you, Eli."

As she said the words, her heart seemed to open up and a breath of fresh air cleansed her pain-filled heart.

A wide smile spread across his face. A gorgeous smile that stole her breath away and turned her mind to mush.

Placing his hat on his head, he took her hand in his. "That's the best thing I've heard since…since I don't know when. *Danke*, Lizzie-bee. You've made me very happy."

He paused for a moment, his long fingers wrapped around hers. She showed a lame smile, trying hard to be positive and friendly. She withdrew her hand, still feeling the warmth of his skin zinging up her arm.

"Will you be ready for me to drive you and your *familye* to church soon?" he asked, still smiling brightly.

"*Ja*, but I'm afraid *Daed* still needs our help to get from the house to the buggy."

"I figured as much. I'll get the horse ready and come by to help you in about ten minutes. Is that enough time?"

She nodded, her mouth too dry to speak. Instead,

she whirled around and headed toward the house. Hopefully her sisters were ready and *Daed* had finished the breakfast tray she'd left for him before coming outside.

As she crossed the yard, she looked up and saw her father peering at her from the window beside his bed. His forehead was crinkled in a troubled frown.

A flush of heat scorched Lizzie's cheeks. Surely he couldn't have overheard her conversation with Eli, but he must have seen him holding her hand. *Daed* might misunderstand and think the gesture was romantic. And it wasn't. No, not at all. But the last thing she wanted was to explain to her father that Eli had merely apologized to her. No declarations of love. No new proposals of marriage. No promises for the future. It was just a simple apology so Eli could clear his conscience before he left and returned to Denver. And that was all.

"Hallo," Eli called as he entered the front door to the Beilers' house. He glanced at Jeremiah's bed, but found it vacant, the covers pulled up over the pillow in tidy order.

The house smelled of cinnamon and he wondered if Lizzie had baked something special for lunch. But where was Jeremiah?

"Eli!" Marty came running from the kitchen, her warm winter coat tucked beneath her arm.

Annie pounded down the stairs, the ties on her *kapp* whipping at her shoulders. Both girls launched themselves at him in a tight three-way hug.

"Oof!" he grunted and staggered back with their

impact, then laughed. "You're not happy to see me, are you?"

"Of course we are," Marty said with a grin.

"Look! I lost another tooth last night." Annie smiled wide, showing a gaping hole in the front.

Eli leaned over to look closely, realizing how much he loved these two little girls. It would be so difficult to leave and never see them again. And what would they think of him when they found out he was gone? He hated the thought that they might be disappointed in him.

"Wow! You've lost a lot of teeth lately. How many does that make now?" he asked.

"Two in the last month. Lizzie says I'm getting my permanent teeth in because I'm growing up so fast."

"*Ach*, I suppose that's true. You're almost as tall as Marty." He glanced between the two girls, comparing their height.

Standing straighter, Marty frowned at that. "*Ne*, she's not. I'm still the tallest. That's 'cause I'm the oldest."

Annie giggled, her sweet voice filling the room. "But not for long. Lizzie says if I eat all my vegetables, I'll grow up to be tall and strong. I might pass you up one day."

"You will not," Marty said.

"I might," Annie insisted.

The two girls engaged in a harmless pushing match and Eli reached out to separate them. "*Ach*, that's no way to treat one another. When you're older, you'll be the best of friends. I promise you that. Until then, be kind and take care of one another."

As the elder, Marty nodded, looking rather serious.

The thought of leaving and never seeing them grow up to be lovely young women brought a pang of hurt to Eli's chest. How he would miss them.

"I'm sorry," Annie said, hugging her sister.

A movement caught Eli's eye and he looked up, seeing Lizzie standing in the threshold to the kitchen. Dressed in her winter coat and black traveling bonnet, she held a large basket hanging from one arm.

"Annie, it's time to leave. Go get your coat," she said.

The girl did as asked, hurrying to the closet.

Eli stood straight, contemplating Lizzie. Her cheeks were flushed, possibly from baking early that morning. Her pale lavender skirts swished against her legs as she reached for a pair of gloves on the table.

"Where is Jeremiah?" he asked.

She jutted her chin toward the bathroom. "He insisted on bathing himself this morning. I couldn't stop him."

Eli widened his eyes. "He's not walking on his broken leg, is he?"

"*Ne, ne.* He's walking on crutches. He promised not to put any weight at all on his bad leg. He knows how important it is to let it heal." The concern in her voice belied her words.

Eli's gaze followed her as she walked down the short hall to the bathroom and tapped lightly on the closed door.

"*Daedi*, are you all right? Do you need any help?" she asked, leaning her cheek against the hard panel.

"*Ne!* I'm fine," came Jeremiah's muffled response.

A loud clatter and splash accompanied his words, lending doubt to his statement.

"Eli is here to take us to church," she said.

"I'll be right out."

Lizzie returned to the living room, tugging on her gloves. She helped Annie with her coat and tidied a short wisp of hair. Watching Lizzie lovingly caress each child's cheek, Eli thought she would make an amazing mother one day. And suddenly, he saw her with new eyes. No longer was she the young teenaged girl he'd loved and left. Now, she was a fully matured woman who understood her place in the world and was confident in her choices.

The bathroom door rattled and jerked open, releasing a blast of steam. Jeremiah stood there on crutches, holding his injured leg up so it didn't touch the floor. He was fully dressed in his black frock coat, his combed hair and beard slightly damp.

Lizzie set her basket aside and both she and Eli hurried to help the man as he hobbled forward.

"Danke," he said.

Eli flinched, surprised to hear such a gracious word directed at him. Not since he'd been home had he heard anything approaching gratitude from Jeremiah. After working for the man for almost two months now, maybe Eli was growing on him. Maybe Jeremiah didn't think he was such a bad influence on Lizzie after all. Of course, that would end if Eli returned to Denver. And though he knew Jeremiah didn't approve of him, Eli hated the thought of losing the man's respect. He hated to let him and elders of their church down. He knew what people in the *Gmay* would say about him. He could just imagine Marva Geingerich's response at church.

You see? I told you he wouldn't stay with us, she would tell everyone who would listen.

He could also imagine his mother's tears. His leaving would break her heart. And though his father would never show his emotions, Eli knew it would break his heart too. But he mustn't let that be his reason for staying. Whether he stayed or left must be purely between him and *Gott*. He would have to live with his decision for the rest of his life and he must make the choice that was right for him.

Jeremiah fell back into a chair, breathing hard while Lizzie reached for his winter coat. One of his crutches dropped to the floor with a clatter while the other leaned against the side of the chair. Eli picked them up, holding both crutches at the ready.

"Vie gehts?" Eli asked the older man.

"I'm just fine," Jeremiah said as Lizzie held up his coat and he thrust each of his arms into the sleeves.

"Does your leg cause you any pain?" Eli asked.

"Ne, it feels *gut*. But I hate this weakness. I can't hardly move without being out of breath. You were right. My muscles aren't as strong anymore." The man wiped his forehead, seeming a bit out of sorts.

"Don't worry. The weakness will fade," Eli assured him.

Jeremiah looked up, his eyes filled with hope. "You really think so?"

"Ja, I know so."

"I must do more exercises, now that I'm able to get up and walk on crutches. I need to get stronger."

"That is a *gut* idea, but don't overdo. Give your body time to mend."

Jeremiah blessed Eli with a coveted smile. And that

alone made him feel incredibly happy inside. But it soon faded when he thought of the stern frown that would cover the elder man's face once he learned that Eli had returned to Denver.

"Are you ready to go?" Lizzie asked her father.

He nodded, reaching for his crutches. Eli helped him as he stood.

"Marty, get the door," Lizzie called.

Both little girls hurried to open the way so that Jeremiah could pass through to the front porch. Outside, Eli lifted Jeremiah down the stairs. He had spread ice melt so the path to the buggy wasn't slick. They all moved at a slower pace, but once Lizzie had retrieved her basket and they were loaded inside, Eli breathed a silent sigh of relief.

Taking the lead lines into his hands, he released the break and called to Billie. *"Schritt!"*

The horse stepped forward in a jaunty trot, as if understanding the happy mood inside the buggy. Eli held the lead lines in his hands and thought about how much he would miss working with horses and the other livestock once he was back in Denver. Already he was yearning for the feel of a plow as it dug into the rich, fertile soil. The excitement of the harvest. The pleasure of eating one of Lizzie's home-baked pies. But if he stayed, he would long for the work he was missing in Denver. The joy of helping someone survive a heart attack, or saving their life after a bad accident. He'd put years into his schooling and couldn't let it go.

Returning to the present, he mentally calculated how long it would take to drive to Bishop Yoder's farm. Once they arrived, there would be many strong men to lift Jeremiah out of the buggy. They'd be happy to help, always working together for the good of them all. He realized how much he would miss each member of the *Gmay*.

As he listened to the girls' happy chatter in the back seat, he was surprised that Jeremiah chimed in now and then. Yes, the man was definitely feeling better. And though he was still weak, he was growing stronger every day. Soon, he wouldn't need Eli to work his farm. Soon, Eli could leave Lizzie and her sweet *familye* behind and return to his *Englisch* life. Lizzie had helped him see that Shannon's death hadn't been his fault and while he still grieved for her loss, he was grateful he'd been privileged to know his fiancée, for however short a time. But he wouldn't let guilt hold him back from the direction his life needed to take. Being a paramedic was what he'd worked so hard for. It was what he wanted to do with his life. He had to go back to Denver. He just had to. Lizzie would understand even if his parents and the rest of the *Gmay* wouldn't.

There. He'd finally made the decision of what he should do. He would return to Denver right after Thanksgiving. It was the right thing to do. He knew it deep within his heart. So, why did he feel so gloomy inside?

Chapter Fifteen

Sitting in the back seat of the buggy with her sisters, Lizzy enjoyed this trip to church more than any other she could remember. Snuggled in her warm cape and mittens, she listened to her sisters' happy prattle and watched the beautiful scenery pass by the window. Tall mountains and wide-open fields covered with snow met her view.

Once they arrived at Bishop Yoder's farm, Eli hopped out to help her father. Without being summoned, numerous men and boys appeared, eager to assist. They lifted Jeremiah easily and carried him inside the spacious barn. Lizzie followed with her father's crutches, placing them nearby.

"Eli!"

Little Timmy Hostetler ran into the barn and made a beeline straight for Eli. The man turned, saw the boy and scooped him up and spun him around before pausing for a tight hug.

"There's my Timmy. How are you doing this fine day?" Eli asked.

Still in the man's arms, the boy drew back and

placed his hands trustingly on Eli's shoulders. "I'm great. Even *Mamm* wonders at my recovery."

David stood nearby, a satisfied smile on his lips. "That's right. Linda thought he was too wild before he got sick. Now, she can't believe how active he is."

The other men laughed, patting Eli on the back.

Nearby, Linda Hostetler nudged old Marva Geingerich. "What do you think, Marva? Look at all the *gut* things Eli has done. Isn't it *wundervoll*? Do you still think he's going to leave again?"

"Humph!" was all Marva said.

Lizzie would have laughed it if hadn't been so sad to her. Watching Eli mingle with members of their *Gmay*, she felt a burst of joy. They were a tight community, sharing one another's burdens and joys. It was so good that they had avoided several catastrophes and they were happy to have all their members here today. But more than that, she gazed at Eli, and a sudden, wrenching sadness filled her heart with pain. Because she knew he would be leaving soon.

Marva Geingerich had been right all along.

Turning away, Lizzie headed into the house where she assisted the other women with the food. Abby and Fannie welcomed her and she pasted a smile on her face, pretending all was well.

When they were called in to church, Lizzie stepped outside and walked to the barn. Taking her place opposite the men, she sang when appropriate and listened intently as the bishop explained the true meaning of *Gelassenheit*, the joy in submission to *Gott*. She'd fought her fears for so many years now, but longed for a calm heart. She'd forgiven Eli, but still felt like she needed to let go of her fears. And that's when she realized the difficulty was no longer with Eli, but rather with herself. Withholding her forgiveness had made her the sinner, but pardoning Eli had taken a giant leap of faith. In spite of her father's disapproval and knowing Eli would soon be leaving, her heart was softened and she finally let go of her anger and doubts.

Glancing over at Eli, she watched his expressions as he listened intently to the bishop's sermon. A mixture of yearning and torment filled his eyes.

Lizzie's heart reached out to him. He didn't have an easy task ahead of him. It would take a lot for him to turn his back on his parents and church and walk away again. To return to his *Englisch* life alone, without Shannon or anyone else to love and care for. Lizzie knew she could never have that kind of strength, but neither could she be angry with him for his choices. Because now, she had another huge problem to deal with.

In spite of her father's disapproval, in spite of her best efforts not to, she still loved Eli more than ever before.

So much for her vow never to let him break her heart again.

The morning before Thanksgiving Day, Lizzie walked out to the barn under cover of darkness. Planning to get an early start to her day, she would feed the chickens first. She needed the extra eggs for her pies, breads and cream fillings.

Crossing the yard, she snuggled her knitted scarf tighter around her throat. As she exhaled, she saw her breath on the air like the blast from a steam engine. The sun wasn't even up yet, but she couldn't sleep. Too many things waged a battle inside her mind. Preparation of her *familye*'s feast, finding extra time when her sisters weren't around so she could sew a new dress for each of them before Christmas and Eli's inevitable departure.

Inside the barn, she looked up, surprised to discover that Eli's horse and buggy were already here. Two tall canisters of fresh milk sat beside the door. Since he was nowhere to be seen, she figured he must have finished the milking and gone out in the field with the cows. But why was he here so early? Maybe he couldn't sleep either.

Going about her business, she removed her gloves and picked up a silver scoop. First, she dug it into the grain, then into the cracked corn before dumping it all into her bucket and mixing it together. The extra protein helped the hens keep laying eggs even with the colder, shorter days of winter.

Looking up, she saw Eli's jacket had fallen off the peg by the door. She stepped over and lifted the coat to hang it up and blinked when some papers fell open on the ground. She picked them up, surprised to discover another letter from Eli's old boss in Denver. The man named Tom Caldwell.

Glancing at the doorway, she hunched her shoulders, feeling guilty for reading Eli's personal correspondence. She should return the letter to his coat and forget she'd ever seen it.

Folding the pages, her eyes caught the words *job* and *excited for your return*. Unable to resist, she quickly scanned the contents, discovering that Tom Caldwell needed Eli's acceptance of the supervisory job with a start date of December 1.

"Lizzie?"

She whirled around and faced Eli, flustered to be caught in the act of reading his mail. "I…um, your coat was on the ground and when I picked it up, this letter fell out."

She quickly handed the pages to him. Never had she been more conscious of her lack of worldliness. Compared to the classes he'd taken at the university and the life he'd lived among the *Englisch*, she must seem so simple and unsophisticated.

He gazed at the papers in his hand, overly quiet and seemingly uncertain. "Did you…did you read it?"

She nodded, unwilling to lie. "I'm sorry. I didn't mean to pry. It was just lying there open and I…"

Succumbed.

"*Ne*, it's me who is sorry, Lizzie. I should have taken better care. I didn't want you to see this." He peered at her, his eyes filled with misgivings. "Are you angry at me?"

She hesitated, her heart filled with anguish. How she hated to lose him a second time. How she hated that he couldn't seem to find contentment here in Riverton. But she couldn't be angry with him anymore. What good would it do? She loved him and truly wanted him to be happy, even if it meant losing him.

"*Ne*, I'm not angry. In fact, I understand." Reaching out, she squeezed his hand and met his gaze with conviction.

"You do?" he asked.

She nodded, but didn't speak. Her throat felt like it was stuffed with sandpaper.

"You see why I want to go, don't you? It's a great opening for me, Lizzie. It's what I've always wanted and I'll never get this chance again. All of my schooling has been for this opportunity. I can't pass it up. You know that, don't you?" He sounded almost desperate to convince her. And for a moment, she thought he was really trying to convince himself.

She showed a sad little smile and nodded. "*Ja*, I know it's what you've always wanted the most. I wish you would stay here in Riverton, but I know you have a gift for helping others. I can't hold you back from reaching your potential, nor will I judge you or try to stop you from following your heart. You have to decide for yourself. And I promise to support you in whatever life you choose, even though my place is here in Riverton, with our people. I care so very deeply for you and I just want you to be happy. Even if that means we'll never see each other again."

Before he could respond, she leaned upward on her tippy-toes and kissed his cheek farewell, then whirled around and raced back to the house. She didn't stop until she was safely inside her room where she closed the door and lay upon her bed to have a good, muffled cry. She would send the girls out to feed the chickens and gather the eggs later on. But even if the house was burning down around her, she didn't think she could face Eli again. She meant everything she had said to him. And right now, his happiness meant more to her than anything else, even if it meant she had to let him go.

Eli stood where Lizzie had left him. He stared at the open doorway, transfixed by the sight of her slender back as she walked away from him. Knowing he would never see her again. He couldn't move. Couldn't breathe. An overwhelming feeling of deep, abiding loss and grief pulsed over him again and again, like the crashing of tidal waves buffeting the shore. Lizzie was gone. All he had to do was finish his chores and go home. And the day after Thanksgiving, he could catch a bus back to Denver. It was what he wanted.

Or was it?

Lizzie wouldn't be there. He'd never see her again. Never hear her laugh or see her smile. Never be able to seek out her advice or hear his name breathed from her lips in a sigh of happiness ever again. And it was his own fault. He'd made this happen. With his thoughtless, selfish desires to chase the world.

But maybe, just maybe, it didn't have to be like this. He had one chance to make this right. To change the outcome. And suddenly, his life came into focus. It was as if a panoramic view opened up to him with his past, present and future life right before his eyes. Finally, he could see it all and understood what he wanted most above all other things.

His heart was filled with absolute confidence in what he must do. But he must do it now.

Turning, he reached for his coat. His course was set. He'd made up his mind and knew just what he wanted out of life. But he better not blow it this time. Because his eternal happiness was depending on what he did within the next ten minutes.

Chapter Sixteen

Over an hour later, Lizzie waited until she heard her sisters rustling around in their bedroom before she went downstairs and started breakfast. Finally the sun was up and she could stop staring at the ceiling in her room. She couldn't lay on her bed feeling sorry for herself all day long. She wiped her eyes and blew her nose and took hold of her composure. Within a week, Eli would be gone back to Denver and she'd never see him again. She had to accept that and move on.

"Why are your eyes all red and puffy?" little Annie asked when she came into the kitchen.

The girl's *kapp* and apron were askew. Lizzie adjusted her sister's clothing before turning toward the stove. "I think I might be catching a cold."

Which was partly true. She'd been sniffling even before her talk out in the barn with Eli that morning.

"*Guder mariye,*" Jeremiah called as he hobbled into the room on his crutches.

He smiled as he kissed Lizzie on the forehead, then scooted back a chair and sat down.

"*Guder mariye, Daedi,*" Lizzie said.

She watched him briefly, wondering if it was too soon for him to be getting around on his own. But since he never put any weight on his injured leg, she figured it was all right.

When Marty joined them seconds later, Lizzie set a meal of scrapple, bacon and thick-sliced bread on the table, then took her seat and bowed her head for prayer. As they ate, she responded automatically to questions and nodded to the conversations around her, but didn't really listen. Later, as she went about her day, she felt like she was moving in a fog. Her bones were achy, her chest filled with a painful emptiness. Maybe she had caught a cold after all. Surely it had nothing to do with losing the love of her life. Again.

"Do you want me to see if we have more eggs?" Marty asked later that afternoon.

Lizzie felt a tad guilty for sending the girl on another errand, but she had been avoiding the barn at all costs. She couldn't see Eli again. She just couldn't.

"I'm afraid I do need two more eggs," she said.

Nodding obediently, Marty did as asked. She returned minutes later with three fresh eggs.

"That's all there is. I hope that's enough to make your pies," Marty said as she set the eggs carefully on the counter.

Lizzie didn't look up from the batter she was whipping with a whisk. "*Danke, boppli*. I think this will be enough."

"*Gut!*" The girl reeled around and headed back to the living room. Lizzie knew she had a new book she wanted to read and decided to let her go. After all, it was Thanksgiving tomorrow. Except for the mandatory work of milking and feeding the livestock, they all planned to take a break from their other chores.

Once her pies sat cooling on the counter, Lizzie decided she needed some fresh air. Wrapping her cape around her, she stepped out on the front porch where she wouldn't be seen from the barn by Eli. Sitting in an Adirondack chair, she took several deep breaths, letting the frosty air cool her heated cheeks. It had gotten hot in the kitchen and she was grateful for this short break.

When she finally turned to go back inside, she glanced at the mailbox sitting at the edge of the lawn. The red flag was up, signaling to the postman that he should collect a letter to mail. That wasn't right. She had placed no letters there.

Planning to lower the flag, she stepped down off the porch and hurried over to the box. Inside, she found a sealed envelope from Eli to Tom Caldwell in Denver.

Her heart sank. No doubt the letter was Eli's acceptance of the job offer. Out of a selfish desire to keep him there in Riverton, Lizzie thought about taking the letter and destroying it. But that wouldn't be honest. Her personal integrity wouldn't allow her to do such a thing. Besides, destroying the letter wouldn't change Eli's decision. Instead, she left the letter right where it was and closed the door to the box. The red flag was up and she didn't lower it. The postman would pick it up within the next few minutes. But now, her heart felt even heavier than before. She'd seen the proof with her own eyes. Eli was leaving. She would never see him again.

Turning, she returned to the kitchen where she forced herself to focus on cleaning the turkey for their big feast tomorrow afternoon. In spite of it being Thanksgiving, she was having serious difficulty counting all her many blessings.

She tried to think of all the things she was grateful for. Her *familye* and their good health. The *Gmay* and all her many friends who genuinely cared about her. Good, nutritious food and the plentiful moisture they'd had to nourish their crops for a bountiful harvest next fall. It was all so wonderful. So grand and glorious. Other than a husband and *familye* of her own, she had everything an Amish woman could want. Perhaps she would one day meet another good man she could love and respect. Someone who would love her in return. But right now, she just couldn't feel any joy. Maybe in the near future. But not today. Not when she knew she would never see Eli again.

The following morning, Lizzie didn't feel much better. In spite of her sisters' happy banter, she carried a heavy heart as she prepared a Thanksgiving feast for her *familye*. In fact, she didn't feel like celebrating. She felt like crying. But the Lord wanted her to have joy, so she pasted a smile on her lips and forced herself to be in a good mood. But deep inside, she felt empty.

While her sisters set the table, Lizzie mixed the stuffing. It was filled with celery, sage and onion, and her nose twitched with the wonderful aromas. When it was time, her father helped her stuff the turkey. Once it was in the oven, she set the timer and glanced over at the counter. Hmm. Where had Marty gone off to? She was supposed to be peeling the potatoes. In fact, where was Annie? She had been given the task of cleaning the broccoli. Her vacant step stool stood in front of the kitchen sink, but no girls were anywhere in sight.

"Marty! Annie! *Kumme helfe*," she called, turning toward the door.

Jeremiah stood there on his crutches, his casted leg held up from touching the floor. She had to admit, she was delighted that he was getting around so well. Because of Eli, the exercises had really helped and she must thank him for...

She paused, her brain spinning. Eli was leaving. She couldn't thank him. He wouldn't be at church next Sunday, nor would he be back at the farm to help her father with his chores.

"Where are those *maed*?" she asked, her voice rather brusque as she dried her damp hands on a clean dish towel. She stepped toward the living room, trying to see past her father's shoulder. He just stood there in the way, not bothering to move at all. Of course, he wasn't very light on his feet these days, but the least he could do was step to one side and let her pass.

"Lizzie," he said.

"Ja?" She glanced at his face, trying to skirt around him.

He lifted a hand and she drew up beside him. Caught between the fingers of his right hand was an envelope.

"What is this?" she asked, peering at him.

She didn't have time for nonsense. Not if he wanted his Thanksgiving dinner to be served on time.

He rotated the envelope so she could see her name on it, perfectly written in Eli's angled scrawl. She didn't take the letter. No, she couldn't.

"This is for you," Jeremiah said. "It's from Eli."

"*Ja*, I can see that." She backed away, turning toward the sink. Trying to ignore the heavy beating in her chest and the sound of her own pulse pounding in her ears.

"He wanted you to have it. Because I hid his other letters from you, I promised him that I'd deliver this one to you personally." Jeremiah's lips twitched with laughter, but she didn't find anything humorous about it.

"I don't want it. Take it away." She made a pretense of cutting more celery for the cranberry salad she was making. Why would Eli write another letter to her? It was bad enough that he was leaving right after Thanksgiving. After all, they both knew he must report to his new job by December 1. There was no explanation required this time, so there was no need for him to say goodbye in a letter too.

Jeremiah hobbled over to her, standing beside her. "Lizzie, I want to make amends for hiding your other letters from you. Please, take this letter and read it right now."

The command in her father's voice caused her to pause. She stared at the envelope, knowing it was a farewell letter. She didn't want it, but realized her father was going to hound her until she took it. Whisking it from his hand, she tucked it inside the waist of her apron and returned to her celery. Tears filled her eyes as she cut a stalk into cubes with a knife. When a new Amish bride was planning to marry, she often grew extra celery for all the many foods she would prepare for her wedding feast. But there would be no such banquet for her.

"I'll read it later," she mumbled.

"Lizzie. Read it now." Jeremiah gripped one of her hands, holding her movements still.

She flinched when she saw Bishop Yoder standing beside the refrigerator. When had he entered the room? And what was he doing here? Why had he come here on Thanksgiving Day? It must be serious.

"Bishop Yoder?" she croaked out his name.

"Read the letter, Lizzie," he said.

Confusion fogged her brain. Something was very, very wrong for both men to be here, pushing her to read Eli's letter. Perhaps Eli had already left Riverton and the bishop wanted her to help convince him to return. But she knew that would be futile. Eli had made his choice. She would not beg him to come home. It would be too humiliating. Too pathetic for her to do such a thing. But her father and Bishop Yoder were still standing there waiting for her.

Dropping the knife and celery stalk into the sink, she again dried her hands, then reached for the envelope and slid her finger beneath the flap to break the seal. She hesitantly pulled out the single page and spread out the creased folds. As her gaze scanned the words, her heart did a myriad of flip-flops. She gasped, unable to believe what she was reading. Without a word, she brushed past the two men and hurried into the living room, then out onto the porch.

Eli! Was he here? Or had he already left the farm? She glanced around, looking for any sign of him. Hoping. Carrying a prayer inside her heart.

"Who are you looking for?"

She spun around. Eli! He was here. He'd been sitting on an Adirondack chair, but came to his feet as he spoke to her. He whisked off his hat, holding it in his hands. In his eyes, she saw a mixture of uncertainty and hope.

She stared at him, her throat too clogged to speak. Confusion filled her mind and she didn't know what to say.

"Who are you looking for?" he asked again.

"You," she croaked.

"Did you read my letter?" he asked, stepping closer.

She nodded, a raft of tears clogging her throat.

"Then you know. I'm not going back to Denver," he said.

She swallowed hard, still gripping his letter in her hand. "You're...you're not?"

"*Ne*. In fact, I mailed my rejection letter to Tom Caldwell just yesterday. I'm not going to accept his job offer after all."

"You're...you're not?" she said again, thinking she must sound irrational and foolish.

"*Ne*, I'm not. That's why I invited Bishop Yoder to accompany me here today. You see, yesterday, when you turned and hurried away from me, something cold gripped my heart."

She blinked, trying to clear the tears from her eyes. "And what is that?"

"For a third time in my life, I was about to lose the woman I loved. And I couldn't allow that to happen again. I was devastated when Shannon died. And watching you walk away was like that all over again. I couldn't lose you too. Not again. I know on my deathbed I won't be thinking about my education or my career. I'll be thinking about you. And what good would my life be if you're not a major part of it?"

She shook her head, not understanding. Not daring to hope she was hearing him correctly. "What are you saying, Eli?"

"Just that I love you, Lizzie. I love you so very much."

The letter she still clutched in her hand said the same things and so much more. She hadn't heard him say those words in many long years. But now, he said he wanted to stay in Riverton. That he wanted to marry her. She licked her lips, not daring to believe his words.

"I... I don't understand."

"I know. I didn't understand myself, until yesterday. You see, over the past couple of months, I've experienced your strength and abiding faith, and I now feel a deep sense of peace in my heart. I could return to my *Englisch* life in Denver and forever lose you and the other things that matter most to me. Or I can remain here and always wonder if I made the right choice. In all honesty, I had planned to leave. But then, I started thinking about all the things I would miss. And most of all, I would miss you more than I could stand. Without you, nothing else matters to me."

He paused, taking a deep breath. She forced herself to breathe too. To remain quiet and let him finish what he was saying.

"I don't want to live without you, Lizzie."

"You don't?"

"*Ne*, I don't. I realize that each of us has been given a *wundervoll* gift. The right to choose who and what we want to be. We both have the option of staying or going. I've finally made peace with *Gott* and I want to stay. Because I love you and my faith more than anything else in the world. This is where I belong. I know that now."

A surge of joy almost overwhelmed her. She could hardly believe she'd heard him right. "Oh, Eli. Do you know how long I've waited to hear you say these things? I've never stopped loving you. I tried to pretend that I didn't, but it was no use. I'm sure that's why my heart has been in so much pain. Becoming your wife and raising a *familye* with you here in Riverton has always been my fondest dream. But…but what about your career as a paramedic?"

He showed a thoughtful frown and looked down at his feet. That alone told her he still felt misgivings about quitting his profession. Yes, he could still help others in the *Gmay* now and then with their medical ailments, but it wouldn't be the same. If he stayed in Riverton, he wouldn't be a paramedic anymore and they both knew it.

"You've worked so hard and you love your work," she said. "I can't ask you to give that up. You say you love me now, but what about five, ten or fifteen years from now? If you must abandon your career in order to be here with me, I fear you might come to resent me for it. I don't want you to settle for something you may regret later down the road. And I don't want you to have to choose between me and your career. I want you to be happy. To feel confident that you have the best life right here with me."

He didn't speak for several moments, his eyebrows drawn together as he considered her words. A heavy sense of loss settled in her chest. Yes, she believed he truly loved her. Maybe he had never stopped. But loving one another didn't mean he would stay. Not if he couldn't have all that his heart desired.

"You and the Lord are all I need to be happy," Eli

insisted. "When you turned and walked away from me yesterday, I knew that more than anything. I won't lose you, Lizzie. Not again. I have made my choice. My work as a humble farmer, future husband and father are every bit as important as being a paramedic in Denver. I will remain here with you. I know deep in my heart that it's the decision the Lord would want me to make. It's what I want too."

"Ahum!"

They both turned and found Jeremiah and Bishop Yoder standing behind them on the porch. Lizzie hadn't even heard them come outside. Through the living room window, she could see her two sisters peering out at them. Could she have no privacy at all?

Annie pressed her nose against the glass pane, looking as if she might cry. Jeremiah leaned against the outer wall, his crutches beneath his arms as he held his injured leg up off the wooden floor. Both men wore serious expressions, their foreheads creased with concern.

"I'm sorry to interrupt, but I think I might be able to clear up a few fears you both might have," the bishop said.

Lizzie's ears perked up at that. Eli faced the two men, but she could see the doubt in his eyes.

Bishop Yoder lifted a hand and rested it on Eli's shoulder. "When you came to see me yesterday and told me you wanted to stay, I was worried that you might change your mind yet again. I wanted to know what was truly in your heart. Since you returned home, Deacon Albrecht, Jeremiah and I have been watching you closely. Of course, Jeremiah has had his concerns. He has feared you might hurt Lizzie again, or draw her

off with you into an *Englisch* life. But it has been our
fondest hope that the two of you might discover you
are still in love, and then choose to marry and start
a *familye* here in Riverton. Now that we know what
you really want, I have a proposal for the two of you."

Lizzie blinked in confusion. What Eli really wanted
was to be a paramedic. What could the bishop have to
say that would impact that?

"The church elders and I have discussed your paramedic training at length," the bishop continued. "You
have done so much *gut* work for our people with your
healing skills. Since our farms are scattered far outside
of town, we would like you to maintain your certifications and continue to assist our people as a paramedic."

Lizzie gasped. Had she heard right?

"I have taken the liberty of speaking with the hospital administrators in town. Dr. McGann and Dr.
Graham have both voiced their support and I have confirmed that they will work with you. They are pleased
with the impact you have had in getting the Amish
to receive necessary medical care. The hospital will
even pay you a fair salary to serve as a paramedic. I
know for a fact that Lancaster County and Pennsylvania have Amish paramedics and firefighters who
serve their people. Our need here in Colorado is just
as great. *Ach*, so you see? When we exercise faith and
bow to *Gott*'s will, He blesses us with more joy than
we can ever hope for."

A halting laugh burst from Eli's throat. "*Ja*, Bishop
Yoder. You are right. I never expected to feel so much
joy. I… I can't believe this is truly happening. I can
remain here and work the career I have chosen, but…"

Eli spun toward Lizzie. His eyes were filled with

happiness and eager anticipation. Reaching into his hat, he pulled out the job offer from Tom Caldwell and ripped the letter in two before placing it in her hands. Lizzie gazed at him with stunned amazement. She barely noticed as her father and Bishop Yoder turned and quietly went back inside the house and closed the door. Out of her peripheral vision, she saw the men pulling the little girls away from the window. Finally, she and Eli had a moment alone together.

"Lizzie, you hold my heart in your hands," Eli said. He squeezed her fingers, his gaze searching hers. "I'm not going anywhere. I belong right here in Riverton, with you. Say you'll be mine. Make me the happiest man in the world. I want us to be married just as soon as I'm baptized. Please say yes."

A movement from the window caught Lizzie's eye. She glanced over and saw her father nodding his approval from inside the house. She almost laughed. So much for privacy. But it wasn't as if she needed his prompting to find her answer. If her father approved of this man, then so must she. Especially when marrying Eli was what she'd always wanted.

With tears of happiness dripping from her eyes, she enfolded Eli in a tight hug. "*Ja*, I will, Eli. *Ach*, I will!"

A shout of delight came from the living room. Her *familye* and Bishop Yoder were inside, celebrating this thrilling news. And what more could Lizzie want? This Thanksgiving, she had found so much to be grateful for. So much to praise the Lord for.

"I love you, Lizzie-bee." Eli pressed a gentle kiss to her lips. His eyes were filled with wonder and love.

"And I love you, Eli. So very much."

She heard the front door open and the squeak of the

screen door as her sisters rushed outside to congratulate her. With Eli's arm securely wrapped around her shoulders, she faced her father and the bishop. Both men smiled wide with pleasure. With Eli by her side and her *familye* surrounding her, Lizzie felt such deep contentment that she was overwhelmed with joy. Truly *Gott*'s redeeming love had mended their broken hearts. He had made them whole again. And Lizzie could ask for nothing more.

* * * * *

If you liked this story, pick up the first book in Leigh Bale's Colorado Amish Courtships series:

Runaway Amish Bride

Available now from Love Inspired!

Find more great reads at www.LoveInspired.com

Dear Reader,

Have you ever loved someone so much that their happiness was more important than your own? In *His Amish Choice*, Lizzie is angry and hurt when Eli abandons her and their Amish faith so he can receive an education in the *Englisch* world. But when she realizes that anger is not of the Lord, she softens her heart and is finally able to let go of the anguish and sorrow that has been troubling her for several years. She is then able to recognize that she loves Eli so much that she is willing to let him go, if that is what he wants. No longer are her own feelings and desires of utmost importance, but rather she has learned to put Eli and his needs above her own.

I know that, as we come to accept God's will in our own lives, to soften our hearts in prayer, and to follow the Savior's example, we can find peace and joy no matter what hardships we might face.

I hope you enjoy reading this story and I invite you to visit my website at www.LeighBale.com to learn more about my books.

May you find peace in the Lord's words!
Leigh Bale

COMING NEXT MONTH FROM
Love Inspired®

Available November 20, 2018

AMISH CHRISTMAS MEMORIES
Indiana Amish Brides • by Vannetta Chapman
While mending a fence on his farm, Caleb Wittmer discovers an Amish woman stumbling down the snowy road with no coat, no *kapp*—and no memory. Now he has one Christmas goal: help her remember her past so he can return to his uncomplicated life...but his heart has other plans.

HER AMISH CHRISTMAS GIFT
Women of Lancaster County • by Rebecca Kertz
When Nathaniel Peachy's brother is injured while his family is away, he must accept help on the farm from Charlotte Stoltzfus. But as they work together, can Charlie prove that she's no longer the troublesome girl he remembers, but instead a grown woman worthy of love?

A COWBOY CHRISTMAS
by Linda Goodnight and Ruth Logan Herne
Spend Christmas with two handsome cowboys in these brand-new holiday novellas, where a bachelor is reunited with the only woman he ever considered marrying, and a single mom and a widowed minister find love, healing and an instant family.

THE RANCHER'S CHRISTMAS MATCH
Mercy Ranch • by Brenda Minton
Single mom Rebecca Martin wants a fresh start with her little girl, so when she hears that a philanthropist in Oklahoma is offering buildings rent-free for a year, it's the perfect opportunity. Falling in love isn't part of the bargain...but with ex-soldier Isaac West, it's hard to resist.

A CHRISTMAS BABY FOR THE COWBOY
Cowboy Country • by Deb Kastner
With help from Alyssa Emerson, his late best friend's little sister, Cash Coble steps up to be a daddy to his baby daughter. But as much as he's drawn to Alyssa, he can't allow himself to love her...because he has a secret that could push her away for good.

MISTLETOE TWINS
Rocky Mountain Haven • by Lois Richer
Returning home to foster the twins she hopes to adopt, Adele Parker partners with her childhood friend, former military pilot Mac McDowell, to start a trail-riding program. And the more time she spends with the injured cowboy, the more she believes he'd make the perfect husband and daddy.

LOOK FOR THESE AND OTHER LOVE INSPIRED BOOKS WHEREVER BOOKS ARE SOLD, INCLUDING MOST BOOKSTORES, SUPERMARKETS, DISCOUNT STORES AND DRUGSTORES.

LICNM1118

Get 4 FREE REWARDS!

We'll send you 2 FREE Books plus 2 FREE Mystery Gifts.

Love Inspired® books feature contemporary inspirational romances with Christian characters facing the challenges of life and love.

FREE Value Over $20

---

*When a young Amish woman has amnesia during
the holidays, will a handsome Amish farmer help
her regain her memories?*

Read on for a sneak preview of
Amish Christmas Memories *by Vannetta Chapman,
available December 2018 from Love Inspired.*

"What's your name?"

The woman's eyes widened and her hand shook so that
she could barely hold the mug of tea without spilling it. She
set it carefully on the coffee table. "I don't—I don't know
my name."

"How can you not know your own name?" Caleb asked.
"Do you know where you live?"

"Nein."

"What were you doing out there?"

"Out where?"

"Where was your coat and your *kapp*?"

"Caleb, now's not the time to interrogate the poor girl."
His *mamm* stood and moved beside her on the couch. She
picked up the small book of poetry. "You were carrying this,
when Caleb found you. Do you remember it?"

"I don't. This was mine?"

"Found it in the snow," Caleb said. "Right beside where
you collapsed."

"So it must be mine."

Caleb noticed that the woman's hands trembled as she
opened the cover and stared down at the first page. With one
finger, she traced the handwriting there.

"Rachel. I think my name is Rachel."

Rachel let her fingers brush over the word again and again. Rachel. Yes, that was her name. She was sure of it. She remembered writing it in the front of the book—she'd used a pen that her *mamm* had given her. She could almost picture herself, somewhere else. She could almost see her mother.

"My *mamm* gave me the pen and the book…for my birthday, I think. I wrote my name—wrote it right here."

"Your *mamm*. So you remember her?"

"Praise be to *Gotte*," Caleb's *dat* said, a smile spreading across his face.

"Is there someone we can call? If you remember the name of your bishop…" Caleb had sat down in the rocker his mother had vacated and was staring at her intensely.

They all were.

She closed her eyes, hoping to feel the memory again. She tried to see the room or the house or the people, but the memory had receded as quickly as it had come, leaving her with a pulsing headache.

She struggled to keep the feelings of panic at bay. Her heart was hammering, and her hands were shaking, and she could barely make sense of the questions they were pelting at her.

Who were these people?

Where was she?

Who was she?

She needed to remember what had happened.

She needed to go home.

Don't miss
Amish Christmas Memories *by Vannetta Chapman,*
available December 2018 wherever
Love Inspired® books and ebooks are sold.

www.LoveInspired.com

Looking for inspiration in tales
of hope, faith and heartfelt romance?

Check out **Love Inspired**® and
Love Inspired® **Suspense** books!

New books available every month!

CONNECT WITH US AT:

Facebook.com/groups/HarlequinConnection

Facebook.com/HarlequinBooks

Twitter.com/HarlequinBooks

Instagram.com/HarlequinBooks

Pinterest.com/HarlequinBooks

ReaderService.com

Love Inspired®

LIGENRE2018R2

SPECIAL EXCERPT FROM

Love Inspired
SUSPENSE

Robin Hardy may be the only one who can help former spy Toby Potter—but she can't remember her past with him or who is trying to kill her.

Read on for a sneak preview of
Holiday Amnesia *by Lynette Eason,*
the next book in the Wrangler's Corner series,
available in December 2018 from
Love Inspired Suspense.

Toby Potter watched the flames shoot toward the sky as he raced toward the building. "Robin!"

Sirens screamed closer. Toby had been on his way home when he'd spotted Robin's car in the parking lot of the lab. Ever since Robin had discovered his deception—orders to get close to her and figure out what was going on in the lab—she'd kept him at arm's length, her narrow-eyed stare hot enough to singe his eyebrows if he dare try to get too close.

Tonight, he'd planned to apologize profusely—again—and ask if there was anything he could do to earn her trust back. Only to pull into the parking lot, be greeted by the loud boom and watch flames shoot out of the window near the front door.

Heart pounding, Toby scanned the front door and rushed forward only to be forced back by the intense heat. Smoke billowed toward the dark night sky while the fire grew hotter and bigger. Mini explosions followed. Chemicals.

"Robin!"

Toby jumped into his truck and drove around to the back only to find it not much better, although it did seem to be more smoke than flames. Robin was in that building, and he was afraid he'd failed to protect her. Big-time.

Toby parked near the tree line in case more explosions were coming.

At the back door, he grasped the handle and pulled. Locked. Of course. Using both fists, he pounded on the glass-and-metal door. "Robin!"

Another explosion from inside rocked Toby back, but he was able to keep his feet under him. He figured the blast was on the other end of the building—where he knew Robin's station was. If she was anywhere near that station, there was no way she was still alive. "No, please no," he whispered. No one was around to hear him, but maybe God was listening.

Don't miss
Holiday Amnesia *by Lynette Eason,*
available December 2018 wherever
Love Inspired® Suspense books and ebooks are sold.

www.LoveInspired.com